"Serros has the genius to create   w
sentences."

                                                                                    ne

"Robust and witty . . . Michele Serros brings a rare authority and confidence to these pages. Like Sandra Cisneros, Gary Soto, Ana Castillo and others, she has a gift for the conversational aesthetic that will make even the toughest nonreader in your family wish this little book would go on forever."

—*San Francisco Chronicle*

"Charming . . . [*Chicana Falsa*] pulsates with the exuberance of an unmistakably original poetic talent."

—*Entertainment Weekly*

"Serros scores . . . [with] richly crafted stories in which Serros invites listeners into her world, her culture, her life as a hyphenated American."

—Michael Quintanilla, *Los Angeles Times*

"[*Chicana Falsa*] encompasses more than the vagaries of Latina life in LaLa; the pressures and yearnings Serros describes are those of anyone anywhere in America."

—*The Village Voice*

"Michele Serros . . . treats her subject matter without a trace of condescension and has enormous affection for her characters. . . . The world she creates in *Chicana Falsa* is one that's unique in American letters."

—Carolyn See

"Get ready to laugh your ass off, get pissed off, cry, and then laugh again. This is the roller-coaster ride that Serros's debut book, *Chicana Falsa*, takes you on. . . . Get on board for an American tale of growing up Chicana in Southern California, complete with humorous ups, poignant downs, and bare-faced truths around every bend. Serros's writing cuts to the chase . . . it is real life, with bold attitude, natural wit, and irrepressible charm."

—*Urban, the Latino Magazine*

(continued on next page . . .)

"Michele Serros is part of a generation of younger writers who are fast breaking past old-school notions of identity and style. Wit and irony are her faithful companions, a tender compassion her literary and spiritual compass. She lets us know that cultural confusion—which is as American as it is Chicano—is something to celebrate and embrace. Her writing is fun, funny, hip, and suddenly sad, but never pretentious—the perfect writer to accompany through tense and troubled times."

—Rubén Martínez, author of
*The Other Side: Notes from the New L.A.,
Mexico City, and Beyond*

"[Serros] is a fierce, funny feminist who brings some serious Chicana attitude to her homegrown work . . . searing, comedic."

—*Metro Santa Cruz*

"Michele Serros paints a witty picture of what it's like being a Mexican-American woman growing up in California."

—*The Source*

"The voice of Michele Serros sings and mourns and dances inside a cultural spectrum of beauty and pain. These poems and stories bloom from a universe that nurtures and represses, that embraces and attacks, that denies and celebrates the paradoxes of her being. Michele Serros meets the interpersonal and cultural challenges of our time with a tender and critical eye, a soothing voice, a fluid emotional insight. . . . Lyrical, sensuous, and deeply sensitive, *Chicana Falsa* is an excellent and necessary expansion of the literary canon of American women."

—Michèlle T. Clinton, author of
Good Sense & the Faithless

"Contemporary literary comadre. Michele Serros is a fresh and energetic writer of unparalleled family stories."

—Denise Chávez, author of *Face of an Angel*

"[Serros's] observations speak to everyone's quest for cultural identity and to the love-hate relationships many have with their friends and family. More important, [her] clever approach to these subjects has resulted in a warm and funny book."

—*The Charleston City Paper* (SC)

Also by Michele Serros

CHICANA FALSA AND OTHER STORIES OF DEATH, IDENTITY, AND
OXNARD

How to Be a Chicana Role Model

Michele Serros

Riverhead Books
New York

Riverhead Books
Published by The Berkley Publishing Group
A division of Penguin Putnam Inc.
375 Hudson Street
New York, New York 10014

Copyright © 2000 by Michele Serros
Book design by Tiffany Kukec
Cover design by Miguel Santana
Cover photograph of the author © by Jack Gould

First edition: July 2000

The Penguin Putnam Inc. World Wide Web site address is
http://www.penguinputnam.com

Library of Congress Cataloging-in-Publication Data

Serros, Michele M.
    How to be a Chicana role model / Michele Serros.
        p.   cm.
    ISBN 1-57322-824-9 (pbk.)
    1. Mexican Americans—California—Los Angeles—Fiction.   I. Title.
PS3569.E733   H69   2000
813'.54—dc21   99-045748

Printed in the United States of America

10   9   8   7   6   5   4   3   2   1

This book could have never been completed without the support, insight, compassion and patience of four women. I dedicate this book to them: Nancy Agabian, Claudia Bracho-Perez, Adela Carrasco, and Reneé Harris.

"It's a strange phenomenon. A Latino or Latina gains a bit of attention, and the next thing he or she knows, the words spokesperson or role model become attached to their names. It's as if who you are and what you've done is not important on its own. You must stand for something greater than yourself; otherwise your accomplishments are meaningless."

—Esmeralda Santiago,
Si magazine, 1995

"I think role models are stupid; it's just another hierarchy, just another way for capitalism to keep us looking up at impossible images, instead of looking at ourselves, our neighbors, or our friends."

—Kathleen Hanna of Bikini Kill,
BUST magazine, 1999

Contents

Acknowledgments

Much gratitude to the following people:

Hanya Yanagihara, your insight and expert editing skills made these stories come alive; members of the suggestion box: Cindy Cruz, Walter Bargados, and Jeff Davis; Betsy Amster, for advice and guidance; Tia Karen, for the nifty threads; Jill Hughart, for being such a flexible boss and understanding the untimely calls of that muse; snaps para Grandmaster Pub Man Craig Burke; the music of Elliott Smith; Gene, for love and support; and Marcella Trautmann, whose interest in these stories prompted me to write them down in the first place.

Special Assembly

First period/Free write

Yesterday during first period we didn't have the spelling test cuz Mr. Evans said over the loudspeaker we were gonna have a special assembly in the cafeteria. Thank God, cuz I'm the worst speller in this whole class.

Anyway, I didn't know what to expect, but later I found out that we had guest speakers, different people from the community, planning to talk to us. We had a cop, a news lady from the local Spanish station, a poet, *and*, drumroll, please . . . Anthony Rivera! Can you believe it? I mean, ANTHONY RIVERA! He's a big ol' star and here he comes all the way from L.A. just to speak at our school! I mean, he's a Michael Jackson dancer and everything and man, I *wish* I could see him on *General Hospital* but I gotta come to this prison every day and our Betamax is already broke, so I can't even tape *GH* anymore!

Anyway, the assembly started out real slow (what else is new?) and the cop talked about safety and saying no to drugs and the news lady talked about where she went to college and then the poet read this boring poem and said she was told she could never be a writer, but she followed her dreams . . . blah, blah, blah, and *then* it was time for Anthony to speak. But I guess he still hadn't got here or something, because last minute they had the school nurse talk instead and she rambled on about how important it is to drink milk because our bones are still growing and during her whole talk, I could see Mr. Evans look at his watch and check the door. And then when the nurse was done talking, Anthony still hadn't shown up, so then they had Mr. Romano talk about tryouts for the soccer team, but there was only so much he could really say. I saw Mr. Evans whisper to Mrs. Regalado and then, wouldn't you know it? Anthony Rivera showed up!

He looked really tired and his suit was sorta rumpled but I mean, he made it! He got us really pumped up, yelling, "Any raza in da house?! Viva el Cinco de Mayo!" Which sorta didn't make sense 'cause Cinco de Mayo was two weeks ago, but, hey, it was ANTHONY RIVERA! So he yelled out this kind of stuff for like ten minutes and he kept saying how happy he was to be here over and over again. To be honest, he looked a little nervous. He kept looking at his watch like Mr. Evans did and tapping the side of the podium like Miss Knudson does when the class gets out of control and he also kept scratching the side of his face. Maybe he was nervous because there were "so many beautiful women in the audience." Ha ha. Then he talked about how he dropped out of school and moved to New York City and lived on the streets and how he'd danced on the street corners and then at some party, he met someone who knew someone who worked for Michael Jackson's limo service. So he starting dating the first person for a while and then he dated the second person and then he moved in with the receptionist who worked at the limo service and wouldn't you know it? He finally met Michael Jackson! And then, he got to be in his video!

Then Anthony did Q&A. That's questions and answers. I saw Margaret Simon ask if he was married and Renee Harris ask to kiss him! Can you believe it? In front of everyone! Then someone asked if he had any children and Anthony just shrugged his shoulders and said, "Not that I know of!" Funny, huh? I saw Mr. Evans frown when he said that. NO sense of humor.

When the assembly was over, I rushed over with all the other girls to meet Anthony and it was like a mob scene. He signed autographs and even Patty Romero's windbreaker. He kept misspelling names and forgetting the date, but the woman who came with him, she was wearing all black and carried this fancy-looking briefcase, I guess was like his helper, and she corrected everything for him.

I guess you can say I learned a lot from yesterday's special assembly. I mean, if you're Mexican, or even Puerto Rican, like Anthony Rivera, and you've dropped out of school and lived on the streets of New York City, you can still make it. You can still be a great role model and be in a music video and someday have someone look over your shoulder to correct all your spelling.

Never Give Up an Opportunity to Eat for Free

I kept the poems in a Pee-Chee folder. Three poems written on college rule paper 'cause that way they looked longer. One of them I wrote in math lab, the other in the quad during my lunch hour and the third one I wrote when Paul R. broke up with me and I had nothing else to do that Friday night. Okay, so I wasn't no Jewel and my parents worked too hard to keep me from living in any ol' van, but I was pretty proud of the poems. I read them during open mike at every little bookstore and in any little coffeehouse around town and Mari and Angela were always in the audience and *they* said they were good poems. But I often wondered, did anyone else get anything out of them?

So naturally, I was excited when I got the phone call. The woman on the other end was from my college and said she got my number from a classmate. She said she was organizing a writers' conference, a Chicana writers' conference. She emphasized *Chicana*.

"We're having writers," she told me. "*Chicana* writers fly in from all over the Southwest, it'll be two days of readings, workshops, and lectures, here on campus. Can I count on your participation?"

Did she even have to ask?

Mari and Angela were happy for me, but surprised.

"How is it she called you?" Mari questioned. "I mean, don't take it wrong or anything and I like your poems and everything, but how did this organizer of this big ol' writers' conference connect with your work?"

"It's a *Chicana* writers' conference," I gloated. "And I guess good word gets around."

The conference was over a month away but already I was practicing. I read my poems in front of the hallway mirror. I typed them up on flat white paper and put them in a new Pee-Chee folder, one that had no scribble on it. I found a cute tank top at ClothesTime to match my lime-green skirt. I thought about shaving my legs above my knees.

A week before the event I get a call from the woman.

"I know this is last minute," she said. "But it looks like we'd like you both days. Are you available?"

"Oh, of course," I assured her. Dang, three little poems and already I was in demand!

"Great," I heard her exhale, and shuffle papers. "So . . ." She spoke slowly as if she was writing while she talked. "We have Michele . . . available . . . both Saturday and Sunday . . . to serve brunch."

What? Did I hear right? Brunch? To serve food? My heart dropped.

"Oh . . ." I started. "I thought, I thought you wanted me to read, to share my poems."

"Oh, no." The woman chuckled uncomfortably, "We've had

our writers, our *Chicana* writers, selected for months." Then her tone suddenly changed. "I'm sorry about any confusion. I thought I was clear when I first called you. I guess, I guess I'm so overwhelmed by the conference and all. Wait, let me see . . ." I could hear her shuffle more papers. "You know on Sunday, we're having an open mike. Are you familiar with those? You're more than welcome to share your poems then."

When people say, "You're more than welcome to . . ." what they really mean is "Look, not only was your name not on our original list, but we never even really thought of you. But to alleviate this feeling of guilt, the guilt for not thinking of you in the first place, we'll throw this last-minute invite your way." There's nothing more offensive than being told, "You're more than welcome to . . ." The whole gesture is really a slap in the face. So I'm sure the woman was surprised by my response.

"Sure," I told her. "I'll be there. Both days. Oh, one last question. Do I have to bring my own hair net?"

That night I complained to Angela.

"Quit being such a big baby," she said as she put up a new cleaning schedule on the fridge. "At least you'll get to eat for free and then later you can read your poems. I mean, there'll be more people at this conference than at any of those ol' fake coffeehouse readings you do. So—what kind of food you think they'll have?"

On Saturday morning a week later I found myself at the conference, donning a regulation name badge, meeting and greeting dozens of Chicana writers, essayists, and poets from all over the Southwest, and posing the imperative question.

"Scone or croissant?"

"What, you don't have any pan dulce?" A woman in a shoulder scarf looked over the pastry platter.

"No, all the kitchen help polished them off this morning with their champurrado," I answered. "I'm afraid you're stuck with either a scone or a croissant."

"Well . . . I'll take a croissant."

The woman behind her then asked me something in Spanish.

I answered her back and continued to scoop fruit salad onto her paper plate. She didn't move forward but instead looked at her friend in the shoulder scarf, rolled her eyes, and remarked in Spanish, "I thought this was a *Chicana* writers' conference and this one here can't even speak Spanish!"

I looked up at her. What was *that* about? What had I said wrong? Did I use "muy" instead of "mucho"? *Rs* not rolled out long enough? Oooh, I can get so sloppy with those. Should I have asked her? A Chicana help another Chicana with her Spanish? I don't think so.

I scooped more fruit salad onto her friend's plate and my face just burned. First I was this so-called writer trying to push my poems on supposedly other fellow writers and now I was this wannabe Chicana trying to horn in on a conference, their conference. I wasn't even worthy of serving Cinnamon Crispas.*

I complained to Angela again. We were in my room watching TV that same evening.

"I'm not going back," I told her. "I ain't gonna spend my Sunday morning dishing out mango crepes to uppity Mexicans."

"I thought they were *Chicana*."

"Whatever."

Crispy flour tortilla triangles topped with sugar and cinnamon. Some people call them buñelos, but my family (and Taco Bell) tagged them Cinnamon Crispas.

"So you're not gonna go," she said as a statement rather than a question. "And now you're not gonna read your poems at open mike? Man, you're sure giving this woman who dissed your Spanish a lot of power."

"I ain't giving her no power." I changed the channel. "What do you mean, *power*?"

"I mean, you were so psyched about this conference and even though you were just gonna serve food, you were all looking forward to meeting all these writers, your fellow *Chicana* writers and you were gonna read your poems and now, because of this woman, you're not gonna do any of it."

"But, Angela, she totally cut me down, in front of her friend. In front of other people. I don't have to take her shit."

"You know," Angela said, "why don't you write a poem or something about how you Mexicans treat other Mexicans who don't speak Spanish?"

"But I *can* speak Spanish!" I reminded her. "And I don't make fun of other people's Spanish."

"Yeah right." She changed the channel. "So anyway, how 'bout write something about Mexicans who don't speak Spanish *well*. That's something you can write about. Besides, I'm getting tired of those three old poems of yours."

"Nah, I don't even care," I told her. "I'm not gonna waste my Saturday night worrying about that woman or this whole Woman of the Corn *Nuts* Conference. I'm just gonna relax."

I grabbed the remote and changed the channel back. "And what do you mean, you're tired of my three old poems?"

After Angela left my room, I worked on a new poem. A poem 'bout how Latinos treat other Latinos who don't speak Spanish well.

My skin is brown,
just like theirs,
but now I'm unworthy of the color
'cause I don't speak Spanish
the way I should.

Great idea huh? The next morning I gathered my three "old" poems and my brand spankin' new one and stuck them in the new Pee-Chee. I was armed. I was ready.

The open mike was held in the college's multipurpose room. I could see the woman, in the fourth row, two aisles ahead of me. She was going through her purse and checking her airline tickets. Man, all I could think was that she'd better pay attention when it was my turn to read.

Thirty minutes later my name was read from the sign-up sheet and I walked to the stage. From the podium I could see her more clearly. I quickly read my three poems, saving the new one for last. Then I saw the woman laughing with that friend of hers. Oh, she must've just heard someone speaking Spanish and caught a grammatical error, *grammaticas wrongos*. I cleared my throat and started reading my new poem. I looked up from my paper and saw that she was going through her day planner with her friend. She was checking off dates and her friend was comparing them against her own pocket calendar. They weren't even paying attention to me! I raised my voice and directed my voice toward her. My fingers clenched the sides of the podium and I was balancing all my weight on the tip of my toes. She *still* wasn't paying attention. I found myself not taking the time to exhale, not swallowing my saliva, things I learned in Mr. Bower's speech class that were very important to do when speaking in public. But all

I could think about was getting the words out, reaching this witch of a woman and demanding she learn a lesson from me. But unfortunately, it looked hopeless. I read the last lines of my new poem and thirty short seconds later, I was done. The woman was now offering her friend a mint.

I walked away from the podium feeling so defeated, the last thing I wanted was idle chitchat from anyone. But then this man, in a tie and glasses, approached me. He looked the boring business type, the kind to pull out standard business cards straight out of Kinko's from his wallet.

"Well, that was different." He clapped his hands together. "Boy, you sure have a lot of anger in your work!"

"Oh, yeah . . . thanks." Was that supposed to be a compliment? Why was I even thanking him? My poems, angry? He obviously knew nothing about poetry.

My eyes stayed on the woman as the man yakked on. She was now getting up from her seat. I needed an excuse to confront her, something direct. Obviously, my poem hadn't worked. If only I could've gotten rid of the man, but he just kept talking and talking. Men, they can be so chitchatty.

"You know, a lot of writers don't use Spanish like you do."

Oh great. Here we go again. And now my first critic was getting away.

"Are you working on a manuscript?"

"A what?" I wasn't really paying attention. I looked over his shoulder. The woman was leaving through a side door.

"A manuscript?" he asked again. "Do you have one?"

"No, not at all," I answered curtly. Was he making fun of me?

"Well, I'm a publisher." He pulled a card out from his wallet. "I have a press, it's a small one, but if you don't have a manuscript . . ."

"Oh." I took his card. It was stiff, beige, and basic with only his name and the word "Publisher" printed underneath in black block letters. I thought of my three, I mean, four poems. I thought of how I didn't even have a computer and how I used the typewriter at school to type them up. I thought about this man, a publisher, who was interested in publishing poetry. My poetry. Did people still do that anymore? If I had a book, I could sell it after my readings at the coffeehouses, I could give it to my friends as a little gift. If I had a book then maybe next year I'd be invited to read poems, rather than be asked to serve food.

"Actually," I told him, "I do have a manuscript. I mean, I thought you meant *on* me. It's actually on floppy, at home." Floppy? That was the right term, right?

He looked over his shoulder to see what I had been looking at before. "Do you need to leave? Is someone waiting for you?" he asked.

I looked after the woman. I worried that I'd never be strong enough to question someone's intent or actions, no matter how much they hurt me. Would I always think about what I *should've* said and then write about it later? How could I ever get my messages across in life?

"No," I told him as I saw the woman leave with her friend. I opened my Pee-Chee folder. "So, here are a few poems. What do you think?"

Senior Picture Day

Sometimes I put two different earrings in the same ear. And that's on a day I'm feeling preppy, not really new wave or anything. One time, during a track meet over at Camarillo High, I discovered way too late that I'd forgot to put on deodorant and that was the worst 'cause everyone knows how snooty those girls at Camarillo can be. Hmmm. Actually the worst thing I've ever forgotten to do was take my pill. That happened three mornings in a row and you can bet I was praying for weeks after that.

So many things to remember when you're seventeen years old and your days start at six A.M. and sometimes don't end until five in the afternoon. But today of all days there's one thing I have to remember to do and that's to squeeze my nose. I've been doing it since the seventh grade. Every morning with my thumb and forefinger I squeeze the sides of it, firmly pressing my nostrils as close as they possibly can get near the base. Sometimes while I'm waiting for the tortilla to heat up, or just when I'm brushing my teeth, I squeeze. Nobody ever notices. Nobody ever asks. With all the other shit seniors in high school go through, squeezing my nose is nothing. It's just like some regular early-morning routine, like yawning or wiping the egg from my eyes. Okay, so you might think it's just a total waste of time, but to tell you the truth, I do see the difference. Just last week I lined up all my class pictures and could definitely see the progress. My nose has actually become smaller, narrower. It looks less Indian. *I* look less Indian and you can bet that's the main goal here. Today, when I take my graduation pictures, my nose will look just like Terri's and then I'll have the best picture in the yearbook. I think about this as Mrs. Milne's Duster comes honking in the driveway to take me to school.

Terri was my best friend in seventh grade. She came from Washington to Rio Del Valle Junior high halfway through October. She was the first girl I knew who had contact lenses and *four* pairs of Chemin de Fers. Can you believe that? She told everyone that her daddy was gonna build 'em a swimming pool for the summer. She told me that I could go over to swim anytime I wanted. But until then, she told me, I could go over and we could play on her dad's CB.

"Your dad's really got a CB?" I asked her.

"Oh, yeah," she answered, jiggling her locker door. "You can come over and we can make up handles for ourselves and meet lots of guys. Cute ones."

"Whaddaya mean, handles?" I asked.

"Like names, little nicknames. I never use my real name. I'm 'G.G.' when I get on. That stands for Golden Girl. Oh, and you gotta make sure you end every sentence with 'over.' You're like a total nerd if you don't finish with 'over.' I never talk to anyone who doesn't say 'over.' They're the worst."

Nobody's really into citizen band radios anymore. I now see 'em all lined up in pawnshops over on Oxnard Boulevard. But back in the seventh grade, everyone was getting them. They were way better than using a phone 'cause, first of all, there was no phone bill to bust you for talking to boys who lived past The Grade and second, you didn't have your stupid sister yelling at you for tying up the phone line. Most people had CBs in their cars, but Terri's dad had his in the den.

When I showed up at Terri's to check out the CB, her mama was in the front yard planting some purple flowers.

"Go on in already." She waved me in. "She's in her father's den."

I found Terri just like her mama said. She was already on the CB, looking flustered and sorta excited.

"Hey," I called out to her, and plopped my tote bag on her dad's desk.

She didn't answer but rather motioned to me with her hands to hurry up. Her mouth formed an exaggerated, "Oh, *my* God!" She held out a glass bowl of Pringles and pointed to a glass of Dr Pepper on the desk.

It turned out Terri had found a boy on the CB. An older *interested* one. He was fifteen, a skateboarder, and his handle was Lightning Bolt.

"Lightning Bolt," he bragged to Terri. "Like, you know, powerful and fast. That's the way I skate. So," he continued, "where do you guys live? Over."

"We live near Malibu." Terri answered. "Between Malibu and Santa Barbara. Over."

"Oh, excuse me, fan-ceee. Over."

"That's right." Terri giggled. "Over."

We actually lived in Oxnard. Really, in El Rio, a flat patch of houses, churches, and schools surrounded by lots of strawberry fields and some new snooty stucco homes surrounded by chain-link. But man, did Terri have this way of making things sound better. I mean, it *was* the truth, geographically, and besides it sounded way more glamorous.

I took some Pringles from the bowl and thought we were gonna have this wonderful afternoon of talking and flirting with Lightning Bolt until Terri's dad happened to come home early and found us gabbing in his den.

"What the . . . !" he yelled as soon as he walked in and saw us hunched over his CB. "What do you think this is? Party Central? Get off that thing!" He grabbed the receiver from Terri's hand. "This isn't a toy! It's a tool. A tool for communication, you don't use it just to meet boys!"

"Damn, Dad," Terri complained as she slid off her father's desk. "Don't have a cow." She took my hand and led me to her room. "Come on, let's pick you out a handle."

When we were in her room, I told her I had decided on Cali Girl as my handle.

"You mean, like California?" she asked.

"Yeah, sorta."

"But you're Mexican."

"So?"

"So, you look like you're more from Mexico than California."

"What do you mean?"

"I mean, California is like, blond girls, you know."

"Yeah, but I *am* Californian. I mean, real Californian. Even my great-grandma was born here."

"It's just that you don't look like you're from California."

"And you're not exactly golden," I snapped.

* * *

We decided to talk to Lightning Bolt the next day, Friday, right after school. Terri's dad always came home real late on Fridays, sometimes even early the next Saturday morning. It would be perfect. When I got to her house the garage door was wide open and I went in through its side door. I almost bumped into Terri's mama. She was spraying the house with Pine Scent and offered me some Hi-C.

"Help yourself to a Pudding Pop, too," she said before heading into the living room through a mist of aerosol. "They're in the freezer."

Man, Terri's mama made their whole life like an afternoon commercial. Hi-C, Pringles in a bowl, the whole house smelling like a pine forest. Was Terri lucky or what? I grabbed a Pudding Pop out of the freezer and was about to join her when I picked up on her laugh. She was already talking to Lightning Bolt. Dang, she didn't waste time!

"Well, maybe we don't ever want to meet you," I heard Terri flirt with Lightning Bolt. "How do you know we don't already have boyfriends? Over."

"Well, you both sound like foxes. So, uh, what *do* you look like? Over."

"I'm about five-four and have green eyes and ginger-colored hair. Over."

Green? Ginger? I always took Terri for having brown eyes and brown hair.

"What about your friend? Over."

"What about her? Over."

Oh, this was about me! I *had* to hear this. Terri knew how to pump up things good.

"I mean, what does she look like?" Lightning Bolt asked. "She sounds cute. Over."

"Well . . ." I overheard Terri hesitate. "Well, she's real skinny and, uh . . ."

"I like skinny girls!"

"You didn't let me finish!" Terri interrupted. "And you didn't say 'over.' Over."

"Sorry," Lightning Bolt said. "Go ahead and finish. Over."

I tore the wrapper off the Pudding Pop and continued to listen.

"Well," Terri continued. "She's also sorta flat-chested, I guess. Over."

What? How could Terri say that?

"Flat-chested? Oh yeah? Over." Lightning Bolt answered.

"Yeah. Over."

Terri paused uncomfortably. It was as if she knew what she was saying was wrong and bad and she should've stopped but couldn't. She was saying things about a friend, things a real friend shouldn't be saying about another friend, but now there was a boy involved and he was interested in that other friend, in me, and her side was losing momentum. She would have to continue to stay ahead.

"Yeah, and she also has this, this nose, a nose like . . . like an *Indian*. Over."

"An Indian?" Lightning Bolt asked. "What do ya mean an Indian? Over."

"You know, *Indian*. Like powwow Indian."

"Really?" Lightning Bolt laughed on the other end. "Like Woo-Woo-Woo Indian?" He clapped his palm over his mouth and wailed. A sound I knew all too well.

"Yeah, just like that!" Terri laughed. "In fact, I think she's gonna pick 'Li'l Squaw' as her handle!"

I shut the refrigerator door quietly. I touched the ridge of my nose. I felt the bump my mother had promised me would be less noticeable once my face "filled out." The base of my nose was far from feminine and was broad like, well, like Uncle Rudy's nose,

Grandpa Rudy's nose, and yeah, a little bit of Uncle Vincente's nose, too. Men in my family who looked like Indians and here their Indian noses were lumped together on me, on my face. My nose made me look like I didn't belong, made me look less Californian than my blond counterparts. After hearing Terri and Lightning Bolt laugh, more than anything I hated the men in my family who had given me such a hideous nose.

I grabbed my tote bag and started to leave out through the garage door when Terri's mama called out from the living room. "You're leaving already?" she asked. "I know Terri would love to have you for dinner. Her daddy's working late again."

I didn't answer and I didn't turn around. I just walked out and went home.

And so that's how the squeezing began. I eventually stopped hanging out with Terri and never got a chance to use my handle on her dad's CB. I know it's been almost four years since she said all that stuff about me, about my nose, but man, it still stings.

During freshman year I heard that Terri's dad met some lady on the CB and left her mama for this other woman. Can you believe that? Who'd wanna leave a house that smelled like a pine forest and always had Pudding Pops in the freezer?

As Mrs. Milne honks from the driveway impatiently, I grab my books and run down the driveway, squeezing my nose just a little bit more. I do it because today is Senior Picture Day and because I do notice the difference. I might be too skinny. My chest might be too flat. But God forbid I look too Indian.

Role Model Rule Number 2

Seek Support from Sistas

I took the page job at *In Living Color* 'cause Kirsty had said the hours would be flex, the pay pretty decent, and I'd get to eat for free in the studio commissary. "It'll be fun," she promised. "You'll get to meet celebs like MC Lyte, Queen Latifah, and Janet Jackson. They're always coming by to watch a taping."

"Oh, I love Janet Jackson!" I said. "Specially on *Good Times*. Remember? And her mom, Willona, the really pretty neighbor?"

"Uh, right. You know, Janet's personal assistant used to be a page."

As a newly appointed representative of Fox Television Studios, I had to wear the exact uniform given to me. The white blouse had a Peter Pan collar, a front frayed pocket, and perspiration stains under the armpits. You might ask why didn't I just run over to Mervyn's across the street and buy me another blouse without any yellow armpit stains. But then it wouldn't really be a part of the uniform, would it? The rest of my ensemble included a heavy navy-blue blazer and a shapeless gray narrow skirt that I quickly hemmed to my knees with duct tape before my shift. I also had to wear panty hose, but I brought my own with me. Thank God. I'd hate to be handed used ones and see what kind of stains were on those. My panty hose were regulation style, nude-colored sheers that gathered at the ankles and lay low in the crotch. No wonder old women are always so cranky.

Jennifer, my other "coworker," wore less of a uniform, and more of a getup: a black spandex body suit that flared out near the knees and elbows in multicolored ruffles. She wore a matching bolero jacket in a Pucci-like design and on some days, she wore colored fishnets. She got to wear a Betsy Johnson chain belt. Once, during the Emmys, I got to wear a red ribbon to support AIDS awareness. She probably made three or four grand a week. I made $125. She had her own parking space where some cute Cuban-looking guy was always parked, waiting to pick her up and take her out for midnight paella. I parked darkened city blocks away from the studio, too embarrassed to let anyone see me in my ratty old Geo Metro, and then drove the thirty minutes home in silence to a roommate in his boxers, boiling spaghetti.

But these were the differences between a studio page and a Fly girl. The contrast between me and her, Jennifer and me.

When I first saw Jennifer I felt a connection right away. Hey, she's brown, like me. Maybe Mexican, like me. Do I detect an accent? Should I ask her where she's from? I have to be careful (see Role Model Rule Number 8). But I rarely got a chance to be close enough to talk to her. While I was up in the audience seating area, counting and recounting the same seats for the live studio audience, she was down on the studio stage, practicing dance routines, joking with Rosie Perez, and drinking diet Coke. While

I was alone, standing guard outside the studio for hours on end praying for any type of human interaction, she was behind the doors of the green room clowning around with Jim Carrey (then *James* Carrey) and Damon Wayans (then considered the only cast member on the show that would someday "make it.") Okay—you already understand the difference in our positions.

I thought if only I had a chance to talk, Jennifer would help me. A brown woman supporting another brown woman in a black world. Remember, it was the set of *In Living Color*.

"I'm thinking of talking to one of the Fly girls," I told Lenny, one of the other pages.

"Which one?"

"The Mexican."

"She's not Mexican, I think she's Puerto Rican. Why you wanna talk to her?"

"Well, see I'm really a writer."

"Aren't we all?"

"No, really I am. I write *every* day. I was thinking maybe she could help me. I mean, I always see her talking to Keenan and sometimes I think of some funny things. Maybe he can use some of my funny things for a skit or something."

"You got a script?" Lenny asks.

"A script? Like what I'm gonna say when I meet her?"

"No stupid, a script. A screenplay."

"No, not really."

"And you call yourself a writer? In L.A.? Listen, remind me to give you a copy of my script when we get to our lockers. After reading it, then see if you wanna call yourself a writer. My little baby's gonna be my ticket to stardom."

"What's it about?"

"Elton John."

"Elton John?"

"Yeah, my two main characters are based on characters from his work. One's Norma Jean and the other is Bennie, like from 'Bennie and the Jets.' Get it? And they have a pet. A crocodile named Roc."

One day I found myself at the craft service table and Jennifer was in between dance segments. She smelled so good, like she was wearing something you just know came from Bath & Body Works. She was wearing a neon-green two-piece dance outfit and the scrunchie in her hair was the exact same shade of green. She *must* have had a personal stylist.

"Hi," I said meekly while helping myself to a handful of Pepperidge Farm Goldfish.

She didn't hear me.

"Hi," I said again. "Hey, that's really a cute outfit. Do you get to keep them afterward?"

She looked at me, popped the top of her can of soda, and then turned to ask the craft service guy, "This damn Coke is warm. You got any ice?"

I guess all that dancing really made her thirsty.

I tried another time to talk with Jennifer. This opportunity was during dinner in the studio commissary. The commissary was a lot like a high-school cafeteria, in the sense that the tables were filled by cast and crew according to popularity. The most popular kids sat at Keenan's table 'cause, of course, they wanted to be near Keenan and Jim Carrey. The second most popular table was where the Fly girls sat. The next chosen area was where the writers, mostly young black guys in Dockers, and some studio heads, a few old white guys in Dockers, ate. Then there was the crew table, where all the cameramen and grips ate, and then, last and most definitely least, there was the pages' table, where only the pages sat.

Now, the seating arrangement in the commissary was not set in stone. A lot of times, kids visited kids at other tables, and sometimes you'd see a Tommy Davidson talking to a studio head at their table or you'd find a grip trying to flirt with a Fly girl at the Fly girls' table, but no one ever came to chat with the pages, *ever*. We were like square pegs, the very square pages.

"My, my," said Garrett, the fifty-year-old new page as he surveyed the commissary for the first time. He sat down to dig into his turkey leg and monkey bread. "This is just like Christmas dinner!"

"Are you serious?" Lenny asked. "Eating on fold-up tables and off paper plates in a room full of strangers? Damn, Garrett, where do you eat Christmas dinner? Downtown at the Mission?"

I didn't get to hear Garrett's reaction to Lenny's comment 'cause I had just seen Jennifer get up for seconds. That was my cue to join her at the food line and pitch my ideas to her.

"Man, the food is so good tonight," I said to her as she looked over the cold pastas. "I just love when Celebrity on Wheels caters. Oh, by the way, what generation are you?"

Too aggressive?

She didn't answer me but instead got the attention of a server. "This risotto is friggin' cold. Nuke it for me, will ya?"

I was beginning to think I'd never have a private moment with Jennifer. Maybe she didn't recognize that I was a brown girl just like her. Maybe she didn't care. Maybe she was used to people always complimenting her. Then one day, I was asked to collect the dirty towels from the Fly girls' dressing room. It was late in the evening after a taping and I knew it would be only her and a few other Fly girls. It would be the perfect chance to talk.

I knocked on the dressing-room door. No one answered. I could only hear hip-hop thumping.

I knocked again.

Still no answer.

I pounded on the door with the side of my fist.

The music was lowered and the door opened.

It was Jennifer who answered. "What?!" she asked, annoyed.

"Uh, I'm here to get your towels." Suddenly I felt like a door-to-door salesperson pushing country-music eight-tracks to, well, Fly girls. "Are you finished with them?"

"Wait." She put her palm out. "You're telling me you made us turn down Big Daddy Kane, just to hand you our friggin' towels?"

"Well I, didn't—"

"Turn Big Daddy back up," she yelled over her shoulder to another Fly girl, and then looked back at me. "Now you just wait here till Daddy's groove is done and then you knock and *then* we will open the door." She slammed the door and I immediately heard laughter.

When Big Daddy's groove was over I knocked on the door again. No one answered, so I knocked again. I could hear a new song starting, but no one had said to come in. I continued to tap on the door a few more times then finally I opened it slowly and discovered they had all left the room through a side door. Their white towels, smeared with sweaty beige foundation and red lipstick, were in the sink under running water. As I collected the soppy wet towels, I could hear their laughter bounce off the studio's high ceiling as they exited through a faraway back entrance.

The next night I complained to Kirsty.

"Well, at least they rounded up all the towels for you. Sometimes I have to wait near the showers and *hand* them their towels. That one Fly girl, the white one with the big thighs, if she drops her soap she wants me to go in and pick it up for her."

"Still, why does Jennifer have to be such a bitch to me?" I asked.

"Don't take it so personally. I mean, she's a Fly girl, you're a page. Maybe she's embarrassed of you, or for you."

"Embarrassed?"

"Yeah. Come on, I'm sure she knows you're Latina and maybe she thinks if someone sees you guys talking, it's gonna make you both look the same."

"The same?"

"Okay, never mind all that," Kirsty said as she opened the door to start letting the audience into the studio. "Just tell yourself she's the worst of all the dancers and she's never gonna be known outside of this show. She'll never be famous. Never."

That night during my whole shift I thought about what Kirsty said. She was right about Jennifer being a Fly girl and me being a page. Once you've put on a page uniform, you're already a target of passive contempt. You're a reminder of how detoured a career can go and what a waste a college degree could be. Everyone knows you're around just to separate Sweet'n Low from sugar, take phone messages, or tape off seats in the studio audience (two, if Heavy D is "in da house"). These are things a ninth grader could do and actually, the whole page experience is a lot like freshman year. You're at the bottom and that'd be okay, I guess, to start at the bottom—if you were still in high school, and young and everything. People would be all supportive and say things like, "Remember me when you go far and become a star!"

But if you were twenty-seven years old, like me, and still wearing a uniform, people don't say that kind of shit anymore. In Hollywood, if you're closer to thirty than twenty, you've already exhausted your chance on going far and becoming a star. You're just floundering and people view you as pathetic. Maybe they know about the yellow stains under your arms.

While Kirsty and Lenny began to take people to their seats, I imagined what it'd be like for Jennifer and me in the not-so-far future. What if one of us was famous, *really* famous, and the other still in a uniform?

Fifteen Years Later

FORMER FLY GIRL: Hello. My name is Jennifer and I'll be your waitress for the evening.

ME: Save the introductions and just bring me a menu!

FORMER FLY GIRL: Shall I bring you the wine list?

ME: What? You think I gotta research what I wanna drink? Just bring me a highball and if you get a single drop on me while serving it, I'll have your job. This is raw silk, you know.

FORMER FLY GIRL: Yes, of course.

She returns with my drink.

FORMER FLY GIRL: Uh, excuse me, Miss Serros?

ME: Yes?

I look up from my copy of Variety.

FORMER FLY GIRL: I don't mean to disturb you, but do you want your dressing on the side?

ME: On the side? Do I *look* like I need it on the side? For God's sake, toss the damn sauce with the greens and call it a salad already. And don't try to camouflage any iceberg under the endive. I do know the difference, you know!

FORMER FLY GIRL: Yes, of course. Oh, Miss Serros?

ME: Now what?

FORMER FLY GIRL: Well, I know you're a busy person but you know I'm not really a waitress, I'm an actress.

ME: Oh really? I haven't heard that one before.

FORMER FLY GIRL: And I know you're one of Hollywood's top writers. I mean, everyone knows your name can make or break a movie.

ME: True, true.

FORMER FLY GIRL: Well, we actually, oh, this is funny . . .

ME: Funny? Funny how? I don't have time to laugh. I'm busy, busy, busy!"

I grab two cell phones out of my Prada bag and dial a different number on each one.

FORMER FLY GIRL: Funny, because we actually worked together on a TV show, back in 1991. Remember *In Living Color?*

ME: *In Living Color?* Was that some kind of How to Paint with Acrylics show on PBS? That name doesn't ring a bell.

I give my home number to a busboy and he winks at me.

FORMER FLY GIRL: No, it was a sketch comedy. I was a cast member, actually a dancer, and, well, I've done a little acting since then.

ME: Really?

FORMER FLY GIRL: But you know, now that I'm older, the good scripts aren't coming in anymore and I was wondering, I mean, since you're a brown woman and I'm a brown woman and I thought maybe you'd wanna help out a sister. I was wondering if maybe you could think of a story line, a part for me.

ME: A story for you?

FORMER FLY GIRL: Yeah, I'd work really hard.

ME: Listen, I do have some industry insider advice for you.

FORMER FLY GIRL: Oh really, you do? Wow. What?

ME: Lemon-scented Clorox.

FORMER FLY GIRL: Lemon-scented Clorox? You mean, lighten my hair? I would *never* want to do that.

ME: No, for your uniform. The lemon scent will eliminate the smell and the bleach will get rid of those yellow stains under the armpits. Do it quick 'cause you're making me wanna barf every time you lean over to fill my drink!

I came out of my daydream and found Kirsty had pretty much seated everyone by herself. "There's still a line outside," she told me. "Can you go outside and tell 'em they won't be getting in?"

I *hated* telling outside people they couldn't get into a taping. They're considered C-list seat fillers who've been waiting outside for hours. They're always told that since they have a ticket they're definitely gonna get in to a taping, but come nine P.M., when the studio audience is filled with VIPs and family members of the cast, we don't need them anymore and turn them all away, after we've kept them waiting outside for hours.

I went outside and announced to the crowd there were no more seats. There were moans, pleas, jeers, and a few middle fingers.

And then I saw *her*.

"Oh, hey, excuse me!" I called out. "Hello!" It was definitely her.

"Me?" she asked, pointing to herself.

"Yes, wait a minute!" I looked down at my clipboard. "There must be a mistake. You should be on the list."

The woman slowly walked over to me. "Oh honey, I haven't been on any list for years. I just thought I'd come by and take a chance, see if there were any seats available. I really love the show."

"Wait," I told her. "Maybe there's something I can do."

I looked at the clipboard again. The seats were filled, the studio was packed to capacity. There was only one seat not taken yet and it said, "Friend of Jennifer's, Fly girl." I immediately crossed off the name and unhooked the thick rope.

"You're in luck," I told the woman. "We have one seat left."

"One seat? You're kidding! That's great, honey." The woman patted my shoulder.

I pulled out a sheet from my clipboard and asked, "Uh, if you don't mind, could I have your autograph?"

"You want *my* autograph?" The woman looked surprised.

"Well, we're not supposed to ask the guests, but I'm a really really big fan of yours."

"You're a fan of mine? Honey, you just made my evening." She took the paper from me. "So what's your name?"

"Michele, with one *L*."

"And how long have you been a page, Michele?"

"Oh, uh, just a short time. I mean, this isn't what I'm really about. I mean, I go to school. I write."

"Uh-huh," the woman responded as she started to write on the sheet of paper I gave her.

Later, after I sat her into the last empty seat in the studio and after the stage lights dimmed and the AD yelled, "Quiet on the set!" I stepped back by the railing, near the other pages, and read what the woman wrote to me.

To Michele,

Life's too short— Do it while you can!
Take it from one sister to another.
Good luck and thanks for the seat!

Love, Ja'net Dubois, a.k.a. Willona on Good Times

First Call

"Hello?"

"Hi, Ernesto?"

"Yes?"

"Oh, hi, this is Michele. Michele Serros."

"Oh, hey there, Michele."

"Hi, Ernesto. Um, I hope I'm not disturbing you, but I'm calling about my honorarium for the reading I did last month."

"Ah, yes, your honorarium. Of course. You haven't received it?"

"Uh, no."

"That was a great night, wasn't it? I just love it when I can give back to the community. So many people . . ."

"Yeah, there were a lot of people. Your house is beautiful."

"Oh, thank you. You know, not many successful Latinos like myself remember their roots. But me, I remember where I'm from."

"Right. So, um, listen, Ernesto, when will I receive my honorarium? You mentioned that I would receive it that night and I know you got busy helping set up that salsa band but it's already been over a week and I'd really like my payment."

"Oh, right, right. Let me see, today is Tuesday, I'll have it out today, so by Friday you'll have it."

"Friday?"

"Yes, no later than Friday."

"Great. Thank you, Ernesto."

"Please, call me Ernie."

"Okay, thanks Ernie."

"No, thank *you*. You really helped raise the awareness of Latinos in the arts."

Remember, Commerce Begins at Home

It was a matter of getting rid of the boxes. Ten large cardboard boxes that weighed over forty pounds. *Each*. Getting them up the stairs to the apartment wasn't a problem. The Takatas, who live below us, had their son carry them up for me. He's got this crush on Angela and it's instant how he uses every opportunity to show off muscle in front of her.

"Is there anything else you need moved or lifted?" he asked once the last box was put in the corner. He glanced down the hallway, toward Angela's room. "You need another jug of Spark-letts?"

"No, that's pretty much it, Arlin." I started to lead him back to the front door. "Hey, thanks a lot."

Once the boxes had made it into the living room, that's where they stayed. For a long time.

"So, what's up with the boxes?" Angela asked me in this annoyed tone one morning in the kitchen. It had been a week with the boxes.

"Well, they're the books," I told her. "I mean, my book."

"Your book?" She marked her initials on the chore sheet. "You mean, the book you wrote? It's done?"

"Uh-huh."

"Why didn't you tell me?" She walked over to the living room and tried to open a box. "Ooh, can I have me a copy?"

"Five ninety-five." I held my palm out.

"Five ninety-five? You gotta be kidding!" She laughed.

"Well, yeah, I mean, no." I suddenly felt embarrassed. "You can have one for free. On me."

"No, I mean, you really gotta be joking. You're selling your poetry book for six bucks? What, so people can decide between you and a twilight feature? Girl, you're selling yourself short." She wasn't having luck getting the box open.

"I didn't write it for the money," I reminded her.

"Yeah," she said. "That's what they all say in the beginning. So why are all the books here? Shouldn't the publisher be pushing these?"

It was then I had to share the certain details I'd been keeping to myself. Details about how the press had folded, and how the publisher, that man in the tie and glasses with the boring business cards, confessed he had one too many obligations to distribute any more books and how it was up to me to sell my book on my own.

"So now," I explained to Angela, "I'm gonna have to go from bookstore to bookstore peddling my books. Can you believe that? You think people are gonna want a poetry book? Like who's really gonna care?"

But Angela wasn't sympathetic.

"Well, I hope they're outta here by Christmas," she said firmly, looking around the living room. " 'Cause this year, I wanna big tree and we're gonna need lots of space for it."

But the boxes didn't move. They stayed in the living room through the end of summer, through fall, and into the holidays. Because of the boxes, we didn't get the big tree like Angela wanted. We had to get a small one, one that fit on our kitchen table.

"Hey, you need help carrying that up?" Arlin called out from his front porch as Angela and I carried the little bush up the stairs.

"No, that's okay, Arlin, we got it."

"Okay, but you let me know if you need anything!"

T& make the boxes less noticeable, I converted them into living-room fixtures. I draped a piece of batik cloth over a stack of three and that made a pretty convincing end table. Another stack of six boxes was transformed into a coffee table. And the last single box made a pretty sturdy doorstop. Make that a *very* sturdy forty-pound doorstop.

Once the boxes were out of sight, under the fabric and behind the front door, I didn't have to see them. I didn't have to deal with them. They didn't exist and nothing was said about them again.

Until one day I came home from school and found Louie, Angela's man, in the living room watching TV. He was on the couch and had his legs propped up against the coffee-table/six-box stack. The corner of one of the boxes was torn open slightly and I could see the spine of my book. I could see my name on the spine. The bottoms of his Adidas were scraping against it.

"Hey, watch it," I snapped while propping the front door with the doorstop/single box. "There's books in there."

"Books? Under the table?" He sat up a little.

"No, Louie, the whole thing's made of books." I lifted the fabric up. "See, they're all books."

"What, these left over from all the classes you've dropped?"

"Ha, funny." I pushed his foot off the boxes. "Look, Louie, I gotta keep 'em in good condition in case someone wants to buy one."

"Buy one? How's someone gonna buy a book when they're under this hippy blanket?"

Louie was right. I had to sell the books. It had been nearly half a year and they hadn't moved. I had sold a few to family, but I mean, come on, that's family. And Mrs. Takata seemed to like it when I gave her one with the rent check. But still.

So the next week I took a few books with me down to my car. Five, to be exact. I looked at myself in the rearview mirror and told myself that I was now a salesperson. I could do it. I could sell anything. I was smart and charming and I'd always done well talking someone into something. I'd sold the L.A. Times door-to-door and those chocolate bars for Little League and one time in junior high, I sold magazine subscriptions and won a trip to Magic Mountain. All you had to do was look people in the eye and smile and use their name a lot during your conversation. *Cake.*

The first place I went to was the great big new bookstore over on Westwood Boulevard. The one with free parking where everyone's reclining on IKEA couches, eating blueberry scones and letting the crumbs grease up the pages of books they never plan on buying.

The store's information counter was circular, with lots of computers and those poetry magnets and teeny little books on how to improve the planet. I went there first.

"Are you the rep?" a woman asked me when I told her about my book. She looked at her clipboard. "I don't have one scheduled for this time. Oh, you're not the rep? Well, usually we work with reps or distribution companies. Where's your ISBN code? We can't sell anything without an ISBN."

"What's an ISB—?"

"It's a universal code every book is identified with and it makes ordering a hell of a lot easier." She looked at my book and frowned. "Hmmm. I've never heard of this publisher. No . . . I really don't think so."

I didn't understand. I had smiled and said her name, but she didn't bite. It wasn't chocolate bars and unlike the *L.A. Times*, she had never heard of me or my book.

A customer waiting to ask a question looked over my way impatiently and that was enough for me. I put my books back into my backpack and left the store.

I didn't think about the books for another month and then one day I came home and found the doorstop/single box was missing. After searching through the apartment I found it in the bathroom. Angela had needed something to put the floor heater on and she thought the doorstop/single box was the perfect height. The weight of the heater creased the covers of the first two layers of books.

"Angela!" I pounded on her bedroom door. "What's up with you treating my books like this? You don't treat books like this! What's up with you?!" I was pissed.

She opened her door and looked at the damaged book in my hands. "What?" she said. "You think your customers are gonna complain?"

The following week I tried a second bookstore. It wasn't as large as the new one on Westwood Boulevard and it didn't serve scones. It was a bookstore that claimed to sell books "by and about women." Maybe they'd be more open to selling a book by a woman they never heard of and whose book didn't have that so-important ISBN label. The bookstore had no parking, so I ended up parking a block away and spoke to myself in the rearview mirror again. "I'm smart, I'm charming, I can sell anything . . ." Blah, blah, blah.

I put some books into my backpack and entered the store. I saw a woman behind a counter. She looked up and smiled.

"Is the buyer in?" I asked her.

"I'm the buyer," she said. "Can I help you?"

Her tone was abrupt and to the point. It made me nervous right away.

"Oh, hi. Uh, I have this new book." I pulled one out from my backpack and gave it to her. "I'd like to give you a complimentary copy. Maybe the owner will want to carry it in your store. You can take it on consignment . . . or whatever you'd like." I pretended to concentrate on an Ani De Franco poster behind her.

"Well, I'm also the owner," the woman told me. "As well as the manager and the cashier, today anyway. I sorta do everything here." She looked at the cover and frowned.

Oh man.

"I can't read anything without my glasses," she said as she pulled her frames down from the top of her head. She looked at the cover again. She opened to the first page, skimmed the table of contents, then read a little of the first poem.

Please, you don't have to like it, just be interested in it. Just say something, something nice. Comment on the color of the jacket, praise the font I chose, mention how thick and nice the paper is. Please, just say something, anything nice about my book.

But she didn't say anything particularly kind. Her words were blunt and businesslike. She looked at the back cover, then the front cover again and then she looked at me.

"Well," she said, "I'll go ahead and take five."

Passport to Cross Overland

It was Tía Annie who told me I shouldn't be a writer. "It's not like it's a real job and really," she said, "how much money can you actually make? This house came from your uncle Gustavo's money and just look at all that tile in the master bathroom, go ahead, look. Okay, so it's from Tijuana, but there's so *much* of it. We even had *contractors*. Tile work like that, you can't pay for it by just writing little stories. You gotta have a real job."

At age ten I wasn't sure what having a "real job" meant. I couldn't comprehend owning my own home or having a bathroom full of fancy tile work that came all the way from TJ. One thing I knew for sure was that I loved to write. Writing granted me freedom. It gave voice to all the opinions I was too afraid to say out loud for fear of sounding unladylike or babyish by family members, classmates, or stupid neighbor friend Patty Romero.

But best of all writing allowed me to escape from household chaos, playground drama, and all those boring *Wednesday After School Special* reruns. Yes, escape was wonderful.

I decided early in life I wanted to be a writer. My mother, on the other hand, was concerned about my career as a future scribe. Would I be happy spending so much time alone, writing and writing? Would I "make it" as one? Would I expose, God forbid, *los secretos* of our family? "You just don't share *secretos* with the world," she reminded me. "Keeping *secretos* secret goes way back in our family."

One major secret has to do with the spelling of our family name and Great-Great-Grandpa Cruz. I'll call him Triple G.C. for short. Triple G.C. was the owner of a small grocery store high in the mountains of Zacatecas, Mexico. One day, a customer tried to steal a pack of Pepsi Light (okay, stories do get lost in translation) and Triple G.C., who was bantam in size and demeanor, grabbed the nearest thing—a baseball bat—to scare away the robber. But after catching the man, a struggle ensued and Triple G.C. not only pounded the fear of God into the robber, but the man's skull as well. Triple G.C. *killed* the man! Holding the bloody wooden bat in his hand (by the way, the present-day Serroses kick *ass* at piñata cracking), Triple G.C. panicked and fled his store, his family, and his country. But when he crossed over from Mexico into California, he also changed his name in the process. He replaced the *C* in Cerros with an *S,* transforming *Cerros* to the acculturated *Serros.* One would think he would have devised a better disguise as a fugitive running from the law ("No, our man is a Messican named Cerros, but this Messican spells it with an *S.* Next Messican!"), but his plan obviously worked. Soon after, his family joined him and Triple G.C. found a new life working as a produce manager at a Food Giant in the south end of Oxnard.

And so it was Serros with an *S* that I believed I would see on the spines of the hardcover books I wrote, a name I would sign at future book signings (see Role Model Rule Number 12), and the name my mother insisted I keep after walking down the aisle.

But when I mentioned my dream of becoming a writer to my best pal, Martha Reyes, she had her own plan to guarantee publishing success. Like Triple G.C., it also involved a name change. She shared her idea with me while we were hiding out in the girls' bathroom, ditching English Comp. It was our only opportunity to relax from dangling modifiers, run-on sentences, and the bleeding red ink from Mrs. Smalley's correction pen.

"Look," she said, "people aren't gonna be interested in what a girl has to say, let alone a Mexican one. You need to make yourself less Mexican, less girl."

"Less girl? Whaddya mean?"

"Change your name!" She placed a whole wad of toilet paper under the faucet's running water.

"My name? To what?"

"A man's name. A nice regular American man's name." She went to get more toilet paper to add to her wad.

"Like . . . Tunlop?"

"No, not a PE-teacher type of man. A distinguished type of man. The kind that wears blazers. Remember that guy who came from the college to talk to us? That kind of man, one with a distinguished type of name. Why not . . ." She threw her wad up toward the ceiling. "Why not . . . Michael?" The wad immediately fell off and landed on the ground with a squishy plop.

"Michael?"

"Yeah." She looked up at the ceiling and got more paper from the same stall. This time she grabbed less. "That's close enough to Michele, isn't it? It's the masculine version."

"Hmmm." I thought it over out loud. "Michael Serros."

"Oh, no, you can't keep your last name. That's your biggest problem. Hey, what's Cerros mean in English?"

"I dunno know. I flunked Goodwin's class."

"Goodwin. He's a dick."

"Totally."

"I think . . ." She squinted her eyes in concentration. "I think it means hills." She scrunched her new wad of TP into a tight ball and held it under the running faucet water for less time. "Why not hills . . . hill? I got it, Michael Hill!"

"Michael Hill?"

"It's the perfect name!" She flung her new wad hard toward the ceiling.

"But how will people know it's me?"

We both looked up at the wad. It looked like it was gonna stick.

"Start telling people now," she said.

But it didn't stick. The name, that is. About ten years later I was in a different type of English class, one called Mexican-American literature, and it was *college* level. Martha Reyes had been out of the picture for a long time, which meant I had no one to hide out in the bathroom with and as a second year J.C. student, I was constantly searching for easy courses that were university transferable. This one sounded perfect. Mexican-American literature? This course was gonna be cake—after all, how many books could there possibly be in this so-called genre? But after reading the course outline that first day of class, I discovered not one writer hid their sex or ethnicity. No one changed their name. I was confused.

*   *   *

The other day I was at Tía Annie's house. While I was in her bathroom I looked around at all the fancy tile in it and I started to count each piece. I gave up after I reached the first hundred and wondered how many words I would need to write in order to buy so many pieces of tile. How many words would it take to someday buy my own house? I thought of how Triple G.C. had gone from store owner to store employee. I thought of the course syllabus I read the first day of that Mexican-American literature class. Didn't you have to make compromises to get what you really wanted in life?

I grabbed a wad of Tía Annie's scented pink toilet paper and ran some water over it. I flung it toward the ceiling, where it stuck to the tile. And just as I thought it was gonna fall off, it stayed, clinging.

Second Call

"Hello?"

"Hi, this is Michele Serros. Is Ernie Chavez in?"

"You mean Dr. Ernesto Chavez, Ph.D.?"

"Uh, yeah."

"No, Dr. Chavez isn't available to take your call. May I take a message?"

"Yes, can you tell him Michele Serros called and that I still haven't received my honorarium?"

"Your honorarium?"

"Yes, I read at his luncheon last month and he told me I would have it by last Friday and here it is Thursday and I haven't received it. Maybe you could check to see if he has the right address?"

"I'll tell him."

"Well, should you check my address?"

"I'm sure he has it. He is a very meticulous man."

"Okay, well, thank you."

"Thank you. Good-bye."

Role Model Rule Number 4

Discard Discontinued Text

I guess I've worn them since I was thirteen years old. At first they were just a simple and inexpensive attempt to look cool 'cause when you wear sunglasses it doesn't matter if your eyes aren't blue or that you don't smoke cloves, or that your lashes ain't that long 'n lovely, wearing shades just *makes* you feel glamorous.

So here I am, already twenty-five years old, and I'm still sporting the things: cheap plastic Melrose knockoffs I found at Venice Beach. But this afternoon I'm not wearing them to look cool or even to feel glamorous. Yeah, everyone might think I'm wearing them 'cause the sun is pretty harsh today. But the sun I can deal with. No, today I'm wearing sunglasses 'cause the last thing in the world I wanna do is cry in front of all these people. I clench my jaw and think about what I read from page 254 in Volume 15, Letter P, as the woman in the brown lace blouse breaks into "Ave Maria" and Father Connor flings holy water over the carnation-covered coffin.

* * *

Volume 15, Letter P was part of the set of encyclopedias my father brought home from work one day. He was a man of uniform, a green short-sleeved shirt and matching stiff slacks, flexing janitorial muscle evenings at the El Rio Library. Some Fridays he'd come home with his arms filled with discontinued books, damaged magazines, and long-playing records; each item was stamped DISCARD in purple ink indicating that the item was considered outdated by the Ventura County Library Association. But to us, my family, they were free, which meant they were still good. You just don't turn down free things.

From that day on, I inhaled every piece of information crammed between the burgundy-colored covers of each encyclopedia. They were an impressive set. Twenty-four volumes in all (M and N were doubled up; X, Y, and Z made up another single book) and published in 1956. But, really, I thought, as my father handed them over to me to look at for fun, how much could facts change in just twenty years?

Volume 1, Letter A was my absolute favorite book. It contained a section about anatomy and featured three whole illustrated pages dedicated to the human body, *without clothes*. So many days, after school, in my playhouse, I showed off the outline of the male urinary tract to all my friends.

"Your dad brought this home from work?" Patty Romero asked, hypnotized by the page.

"Yeah," I bragged.

"Man, you're lucky," Goony added. "All my dad brings home is a lousy headache."

But it was in Volume 15, Letter P that I learned about Psychology, or more importantly, Social Maturity. There, on page 254, was a black-and-white photo of a young girl in her bedroom, lying across the bed. She was alone holding a handkerchief to her eyes and she was crying. The caption underneath read, "A mature person does not cry in public. A mature person waits until they are in private to express their emotions."

More than anything, I wanted to be mature. As an aspiring teenager, I still found myself wobbling in my sister's platforms and my attempts with liquid eyeliner still had that inexperienced crooked look. I feared I would never be viewed as a mature young woman. So after reading page 254 in Volume 15, Letter P, I thought that if not crying in public made you mature, then that's what I could do. Simple enough.

But on some days, the tears couldn't help but trickle out and so on those particular days, days I thought I might cry, I wore the sunglasses. I wore some the week after witnessing Robert G. skate the Couples Only skate with Stefanie De la Torre and I wore a pair the whole month after Mama Kitty was hit by a speeding moped. Yes, sunglasses were the perfect accessory for the up-and-coming mature thirteen-year-old.

Twelve years later I found myself wearing a pair the day everyone gathered in the H wing of Community Memorial Hospital. We were all camped out in the waiting room; Alma, Alfonso, Lydia, my father, and oh, too many people to name, waiting to hear good news about a woman who was really bad off. Even though they were all family, and even though we were all indoors, I still wore the sunglasses. I didn't want anyone to see me crying.

"Michele, it's your twenty."

This is how the visits with my sick mother went. Private time, one at a time, that lasted a short twenty minutes. That was the hospital rule.

When I entered my mother's curtained area in the ICU, I

pushed my sunglasses to the top of my head. There was no way any tinted plastic was gonna come between my mother and me. I'm no doctor, but I've watched enough episodes of *GH* to know when someone is really sick, and I could tell she was very sick. Her face was blank, and yellow, and her eyes, half-closed, were smeared with clear gel to help maintain their moisture. Large white heavy-looking machinery hummed over her that displayed discouraging data and charted a losing battle.

I sat near the head of my mother's bed and took her hand with both of mine. Its temperature shocked me. I held it between mine and rubbed. I looked at her fingers and remembered them once filling hundreds of fortune cookies with a junior-high-school campaign slogan ("Confucius say: Vote for Michele!"), the same fingers that typed term papers for me, the hands that laid brick designs for the fancy patio in our backyard and that lovingly pulled my favorite hot chicken pot pies out from our oven. So many things those hands did when they were healthy, active, and warm.

"Hey, Mama," I whispered. "Hey, you look great. You look so much better."

When people are classified as being semicomatose, you gotta remain positive and upbeat 'cause you never know what they may overhear. Negative comments could make them feel hopeless and they may just give up and *leave*. The last thing I wanted was for my mother to leave. I stretched my eyebrows upward and tried to concentrate on not crying. I thought of the sunglasses on top of my head, but the last thing I was gonna do was put them on. I stayed with my mother for my allotted twenty minutes and tucked the peach-colored blanket under the sides of her thin pale body. I squeezed her cold hand one more time before I left.

"*Any* changes?" Angela asked when I came back to the waiting room. She got up from the couch and was already holding her car keys. I had forgotten we planned to have lunch together and suddenly I was so hungry. I realized I hadn't eaten in almost two full days.

"Nothing," I told her. "No changes."

"Well, let's go to Marie Callender's," she suggested, trying to sound positive and in-charge. "I think some food will make you feel good."

"Good?"

"Well, at least a little better." She looked uncomfortable. She pushed the elevator button and rubbed my shoulder as we waited for the doors to open. I clenched my jaw tighter.

Once we were in her car and leaving the parking lot, I pulled down the sun visor and reached for my sunglasses. They weren't on top of my head.

"Wait," I called out.

"What's wrong?"

"My glasses. I left them . . ." Then I remembered. "I left them on the nightstand with my mom."

"Get 'em later," Angela said as she started onto the street. "You don't really need them, do you?"

"No, I mean, yeah I do. I feel like shit and I don't wanna go out like this. I gotta go get them. It'll only take a second."

Angela turned back into the hospital's parking lot and I got out of the car and ran back to the building. I took the elevator back to the third floor.

"What's wrong?" Aunt Lydia asked when she saw me run back into the waiting room. "I thought you were going to lunch with your roommate."

"I forgot my glasses."

"You came all the way back for sunglasses?"

"I need to get back into the ICU. Is someone with her?"

"No, Emma just came out. But be quick, 'cause her father wants to see her and it's his turn next."

I went into the ICU and saw my sunglasses on her nightstand near the Kleenex box and plastic water pitcher, just where I had left them. I leaned over to get them.

"It's just me, Mama," I whispered. "I forgot something." I squeezed her hand and was getting up to leave, when I felt it. She squeezed my hand back.

"You're always forgetting something," she whispered softly.

I turned around and I couldn't believe it. My mother's eyes were now completely open and she was awake. She was alert and actually communicating with me. "Oh, my God." I continued to squeeze her hand. "You're talking!"

"Of course I'm talking. Hey," she whispered, "you're hurting my hand."

"Oh, sorry." I immediately let go of it. "But you were in . . . you've been out for days, they said that you were—"

"They don't know what they're talking about."

I couldn't believe it. My mother was awake. She was actually having a conversation with me! The data displayed higher numbers and that once-dreaded digital line behind her now revealed slopes.

"I'm gonna go get the nurse." I started to get up from the chair.

"No, wait," she whispered. "I wanna talk, just me and you."

"But shouldn't—"

"Where were you off to earlier?" she interrupted.

"Well, I was gonna go have lunch with Angela, but don't you think—"

"Your roommate, right?" she asked quickly. "Where were you going?"

"Uh, Marie Callender's, what does—"

"Oh, I love Marie Callender's. Their pasta primavera is so good."

"Yeah, but, Mama . . ." I tried to change the subject back to her health, but it was no use. She had already pulled me into her conversation.

"You know, pasta primavera means spring pasta in Italian," she continued. "Bobby's daughter told me that. She went to Italy, remember?"

"Yeah." I rolled my eyes. "How could everyone not know? She sent postcards every day!"

"Yeah, she's a little show-offy, huh?" My mother smiled. "You know, I want to go to Italy."

"You do?" I sat back on the chair. "You never brought that up before."

"I decided when I get out of here, that you and I should go to Italy. Let's go to Italy."

"Mama, I think you should concentrate on getting better."

"You know." She leaned closer to me. "When you left earlier, the doctor came in and said I was already so much better."

"The doctor said that? Which doctor? When did he say that?"

"He said I should be out by next week."

"Next week?" I was actually beginning to feel light-headed. "How come he—"

"Wait, wait, listen," she interrupted. "I have some money, a little saved up, so I say let's go to Italy this summer. Listen, I want to go. Tell me you'll go, just me and you."

"Of course I wanna go to Italy, but—"

"Promise, this summer."

"Yeah, this summer, but wait—"

"So, why did you come back?" she interrupted again.

"I forgot my sunglasses."

"You came back all the way just for sunglasses?" She suddenly started coughing.

I poured her some water from the pitcher and she continued to cough until she drank from the cup. "You can't go one hour without those sunglasses." She cleared her throat. "Put 'em on. Let me see you in them."

I put the sunglasses on.

"They're too big for your face," she said.

"I like them like this."

"You look like a movie star."

"Like an *Italian* movie star?" I joked.

"You never know what could happen once we get there!" She laughed softly. "Now listen, you go have lunch with Angela and I want you to buy one of those travel books. Get one on Italy and I want you to come back here and we're gonna plan our trip."

I didn't get up from the chair right away. I wanted to look at my mother. Her face was full of color and actually glowed with life. She looked back at me and smiled. My mother was better. She was definitely going to live. I leaned over, kissed her forehead, and squeezed her hand. It was warm.

The next thing I knew was being woken up by a nurse. I had accidentally fallen asleep on the chair while talking to my mother. None of the nurses knew if I had just gone over my twenty or if I had actually fallen asleep. They couldn't tell 'cause I had on my sunglasses. I never made it back to the parking lot to meet Angela for lunch and my mother and I, well, we never got to plan our trip to Italy. By the time the nurse had shaken my shoulder, my mother had fallen back into a coma. And over three days her face returned to its yellow hue and her eyes returned to being half-closed. We were all relegated back to twenty-minute individual visits and I became dependent on my sunglasses again. And then the waiting game continued. We waited and waited to hear any bit of good news, but it never came. The morning of the fourth day, my mother died.

And so here I am wearing the sunglasses. The same sunglasses I left on her nightstand. Everyone says there was no way I could've possibly had such a conversation with my mother. Everyone swears she was completely comatose and that I must've dreamed the whole thing. "You were tired," my aunt Emma tried to explain. "You hadn't eaten in almost two days and you just imagined she talked with you." But I refuse to listen to her or anyone else in my family. I know my mother spoke, just with me. I look at the woman in the brown blouse and concentrate on her singing "Ave Maria." The lyrics are partly in Latin and I think of Italy and how my mother finally did leave.

I feel my eyes begin to fill with tears and I immediately remember page 254 in Volume 15, Letter P. I adjust my sunglasses closer to my head and clench my jaw tighter as I think about how long it'll be before I can get home so I can go to my room, lie across my bed, and cry in private.

The Big Deal

"So just how long is his hair?" Auntie Alma asked.

I tried to envision a picture she would understand. An image she would appreciate. Jesus? Too heavy. Che Guevara? Too commercial. I needed something more within our cultural grasp.

"Okay," I said. "You know Cher, right?"

Alma smirked. "Of course I know her. Not personally, but I know who she is. I've had a subscription to *People* since it first came out. Don't tell me his hair's as long as hers."

"No, not that long," I assured her. "But you remember her second husband?"

"The one who wore makeup and had the long tongue?"

"No, not him. She was never married to him. I'm talking about Greg, Greg Allman, her second husband."

"The blond one?"

"Yeah," I said. "So Doze's hair looks just like his. He's also got a little soul patch, fuzz on his chin, too."

"Oh, I know what he looks like now." She opened the top cupboard and searched for something. "That's long. Why does he have such long hair?"

"He's always had it that way."

"Well, I guess it's all right. I mean, Jesus had long hair. And most men, when they have long hair, it's always really pretty. Why is that anyway?"

"I dunno," I agreed. "But you're right."

The questions surrounding my new boyfriend were getting more personal, more in-depth, and this made me nervous. Since my mother died, I saw Auntie Alma as the primary maternal figure in my life. I wanted her approval badly, and more than anything, I wanted Doze, my new boyfriend, to be accepted by the whole family . He was due at Alma's in less than an hour to meet everyone—Alma, Auggie, Uncle Charlie . . . the whole crew. I was in Alma's kitchen helping make more food, last minute, as usual.

"And he's definitely *güero,* huh?" Alma asked as she handed me a glass cup full of rice.

"Yeah."

"Just how white?"

"Okay, you know Izzy?"

"Charlie's youngest daughter, Icela, or Icela up north?"

"Izzy up north."

"He's not as white as her!"

"As white as her stomach." I paused. "In the wintertime." We both cringed at the thought.

"Oh, my God, that is white."

"Yeah, I know." I poured the rice in the pan.

"So you must really like him," she said.

"Yeah." I smiled. "A lot."

"So." She lowered the flame under the pan. "Robert tells us he's got some tattoos."

"Just a few, like on his back and arms."

"Any near here?" she asked suspiciously, and pointed to the webbing between her thumb and pointer finger.

"No, why?"

"Nothing." She added some onion-soup mix to a carton of sour cream and started mixing.

"He wasn't ever in jail, was he?" she asked.

"Well . . ." Shit. Just how honest should I be? I ended up confessing. "Not really jail, per se."

"What do you mean, *per se?*"

"I mean, he spent a few months in juvie."

"A few months! In juvenile hall? What'd he do?"

"Oh, it was just some stupid thing. I mean, he was still in high school and it was only juvie."

"Yeah, but a few months, he must have had priors," she answered nonchalantly. "I saw *American Me*. That's the way it really is."

"Now, how would you know something like that?" I asked.

"Michele," she said firmly, "I have the *video*."

"Anyway," I added quickly. "He's mended his ways since then. I mean, he was way younger back then and he knows right from wrong. I mean, he's a pretty spiritual guy."

"Oh, like Catholic?" She pulled out a beige rubber spatula from the drawer and helped me stir the rice.

"No, Alma." I laughed. "He's far from Catholic."

"What do you mean?"

"I mean, he's spiritual and everything, but he's agnostic."

"He's what?"

"Agnostic. He just needs more proof there is a God. He has his doubts."

"What! Oh, my God. I can't . . . I don't believe this!" She looked up toward the ceiling and made the sign of the cross quickly. "Shhh! Don't ever say that again in my house."

"Oh, come on, Alma." I put a lid on the rice. "Half the family doesn't even go to church."

"Shhhh!" she said as she pointed to the ceiling again. "He doesn't need to know that. Stop it. Just be quiet!"

I walked around the counter and pulled up a kitchen stool. I folded my hands together on the counter, rested my chin on them, and exhaled quietly. I felt uncomfortable, nervous. And then I suddenly felt sad. If my mother was alive there would be fewer questions, less negative comments. If my mother was alive there'd be more acceptance and I wouldn't be defending a new boyfriend an hour before his arrival. I dreaded the thought of Doze coming to dinner at Alma's. Maybe it was much too early for such formalities, but now it was too late to call and cancel. He was already on his way. I noticed a frown on Alma's face as she counted forks and knives. I knew she was disappointed by the information she had just learned about Doze. I looked at the kitchen clock. Maybe it wasn't too late to call him and cancel.

Alma stopped counting silverware and came over toward me. She put an arm around my shoulders.

"You know," she said. "All these things 'bout Doze aren't important. What's important is how you feel. If you love him that's the only thing that's worth feeling. Because let me tell you, love comes around rarely. I mean real honest-to-goodness love—you have to grab it when you can."

"Really?" I put my hand over hers.

"Really. All these things, him having long hair, being locked up, not believing in God"—she made the sign of the cross again—"I guess, all these things really don't matter to us, to family. I mean, we're not the ones in love with him. Besides, all these little things are sorta superficial."

"Yeah?"

"Yeah, and believe me, your mother would be so happy that you're happy." She squeezed my shoulder. "Oh, you're so tense. Look, why don't you go over to B&D and get some more sodas, get some more beer if you want." She squeezed my shoulder one more time and walked away from the counter. "We still have another half hour."

"Yeah, I'll run over to B&D." I relaxed both my shoulders. "I also gotta get some salad fixings, some stuff for Doze to eat."

"To eat?" Alma whipped around. "Why? Look at all this food I've made!"

"I know, but Doze really can't eat much of it."

"What do you mean? He's not feeling well?"

"No, it's just—"

" 'Cause you know I make the best chicken soup."

"Yeah, I know, it's just—"

"Wait, don't tell me." She put her hand over her heart. "He doesn't like Mexican food."

"No, no. He loves it. It's just Doze doesn't eat meat, he's vegan."

"He's what?"

"Vegan; it's like a strict vegetarian."

"Vegetarian? You never told me that."

"I didn't think it was a big deal."

"Not a big deal? How can you leave out such an important detail?"

"Alma, it's not a big thing. In fact, his whole family doesn't eat meat or cheese. They don't drink milk either. He was raised that way."

"And he told you this or did you have to find out on your own?"

"Alma, of course he told me. I mean, our first date, we went out to dinner and yeah, he told me right away."

"And you still accepted him like that?"

"Accepted who what way?" Just then Auggie and Benny walked into the kitchen.

"Michele's new friend," Alma told them. "Did you know he was a vegan, a strict vegetarian?"

"What kind a man," Auggie asked, "doesn't eat meat?"

"Hey, you remember the Calverts next door?" Benny dipped his fingers into the beans and pulled out a thick chunk of bacon fat. "They were vegetarians. They had a big ol' vegetable garden and everything. The biggest garden on the whole block and Mr. Calvert still died. They weren't all that healthy."

"What kind of man eats just vegetables?" Auggie repeated. "I mean, where does he get his *ganas* from? Those little broccoli crowns?" Then he and Benny laughed together as they left for the backyard.

"They're called florets," I called out to him. "Alma, please tell him what we just talked about."

"I don't know." She hesitated. "I mean, personally, I just think it's unnatural, strange."

"Alma, what about all this talk about love, and acceptance, and how important it is to find someone you care about in life?"

"That was before you told me he and his family were vegans."

"Alma, you gotta be kidding."

"Okay, tell me this." She looked at the pan on the stove. "He'll eat my rice, right?"

"Well, no."

"But everyone loves my rice."

"I know, but you put lard in it."

"That's not meat."

"I know, but it's animal fat."

"Oh, so now you're suddenly too good for my rice." She put her dish towel to her face and it looked like she was gonna cry.

"Alma, please, what's the big deal?"

"It's just," she said between what sounded like sobs, "it's just . . . I'm so confused!"

"About what?"

"What we're gonna serve."

"What do mean what we're gonna serve? Serve what you've already had planned. I'm just gonna get a few more things at the store."

"No, not what I'm gonna serve tonight."

"Then, where? What are you talking about?" Now I was getting confused.

"What am I gonna serve at the wedding?"

"Wedding? What are you taking about?"

"It's just that since you were a little girl, your mother always dreamed that someday you would meet a nice boy, a nice Mexican boy, and you'd have a big Catholic wedding and we'd, we'd . . ."

"You'd what?"

"We'd have lots and lots of tri tip, Santa Maria style, and now, the more you tell me about this Doze, it's becoming less and less of a dream. I could accept he isn't Mexican, that he doesn't believe in God, but that he and his whole family don't eat meat, won't eat tri tip?"

Just then the doorbell rang.

"So what, he's an early bird, too?" She took off her apron and started for the front door. "You didn't tell me that either!"

I pulled her back. "What do you mean tri tip Santa Maria style?"

"I mean, Santa Maria style, how Vincente makes it."

"Uncle Vincente?"

"That's the way he makes it. Your mother had specifically asked him to make it for your wedding."

The doorbell rang again.

"And he said yes?"

"Of course."

Ever since I was a little girl, I've grown up eating tri tip at almost every barbecue, wedding, and family reunion. The leftovers were relegated to a wonderful week of tri tip sandwiches, tri tip burritos, and savory tri tip toppings for Top Ramen. Now, for those of you not in the know, tri tip is the triangular-shaped tips of beef loin. It can be a tough piece of meat if you don't know how to cook it right and some people make the mistake of removing all the fat before cooking, but if you put the fat side on the fire first, its moisture penetrates the meat and makes for the most super-tender cut of beef you've ever had in your life. Uncle Vincente's way of preparation is traditional Santa Maria style, which means he first sears the lean part of the meat over the grill for like five to eight minutes. That seals in all the juices, then he flips the whole thing over to the fat side for thirty-five minutes, then when the juice seeps from the top of that side, it's time to flip it over again for another thirty-five minutes. The whole process is pretty time-consuming and no one really wants to be over a hot grill, timing the flipping of meat, but here the burden was being selflessly offered for my future wedding feast.

"Vincente hasn't made tri tip like that in years." I told Alma.

"Since Vivian's wedding," she reminded me. "In 1979. He said it was all too much of a bother but he said he'd do it for you. But if your future family doesn't eat meat . . . I don't know what to say." She walked over to answer the door but I pulled her back.

"It's a pretty big deal for Vincente to make tri tip Santa Maria style."

"A very big deal," she agreed.

"You know, maybe it is too soon to have Doze over, to meet family," I told Alma. "I mean, what's the rush? What's the big deal?"

"Yeah, what *is* the big deal?" Alma agreed.

And with that, we both stood on the other side of her front door. Neither one of us moved to acknowledge Doze's impatient knocks and doorbell rings. I put my finger over my lips and Aunt Alma nodded. We stayed quiet until we finally heard Doze retreat back down Alma's walkway to get in his car.

We watched his car slowly drive away from behind the sheer curtains of her living-room window. Alma put her arm around my shoulder again and asked softly, "And what the hell kind of name is Doze, anyway?"

Role Model Rule Number 5

Respect the 1 Percent

During the holidays it's expected that families, no matter how harmonious or not, spend time with one another. If you have a traditional Mexican family like mine, it's an excuse to get together, ditch the Suddenly Salad mix and anything Swanson, and devour homemade moist or dry (depending on who made them) pork tamales. It's a time to join together and sigh with relief upon discovering that every gift box has a receipt on the bottom. It's a ritual to observe Great-aunt Lydia as she turns up the TV volume to high and lowers the iron's setting to low so the annual pressing of used Christmas wrap can begin. "Now this piece is just beautiful," she'll remark, holding a large piece of red foil wrap. "See how it glistens with the TV? Ricky should've been more careful taking this off."

But one year, 1996 to be exact, was different. I can still recall the warm balmy California Christmas night that I spent alone.

I spent it alone because not only was I emotionally overcome and completely outraged by my family's actions, but I was the sole participant in an annual boycott. Relatives who I'd thought were a loyal tight loving circle of kinship actually went and did it. Went against the wishes of a dead man—a family member, I might add—and stabbed him in the back on the holiest of all calendar days. They actually got into their Hondas, drove across town, and chose her over him. Chose to support *her* business endeavor rather than respect the One Percent's artistic effort. God, I'm so ashamed to admit it, but my family actually chose to spend the last hours of Christmas night with Madonna. Not the Virgin Mary, mother of Jesus Christ, not My Donna, the Benifields' twenty-year-old Palomino that had just given birth to twin foals, but *Madonna.* Yes, that one. That new film of hers, *Evita,* premiered nationwide and, wouldn't you know it, landed in a minimall theater smack in the middle of Oxnard.

"How can you go?" I protested as they searched the *Ventura County Star* for show times. "What about our promise to Uncle Charlie?"

"Who cares about that old promise?" my cousin Gina said as she looked for her car keys. "He made such a big deal about everything, anyway. It's a movie, a musical, it's *Madonna.*"

"You know," my aunt Margaret remarked as she caught herself in the living-room mirror, "I could have been Evita in my college musical. Remember that, Lennie? I had the voice of a choir girl. I almost had the role, too, but they said my hips were too wide and that I didn't look Latin enough, not like *Madonna.*"

And that would have been Uncle Charlie's point. Uncle Charlie was my father's oldest cousin, a struggling actor during the sixties and the seventies and even during the early eighties. He never found an acting gig. As a third-generation Mexican, he was always told he looked too brown or not brown enough, too Mexican, yet not Latin enough.

"You know," he'd say, "all the Latinos in this country, heading political offices and creating careers with dishwater hands, but you never hear our stories, see our lives on the big screen. We're almost the largest minority in this country and we barely make up one percent on film!"

Unfortunately, Uncle Charlie's last role five years ago was as a dying man at Ventura Community Memorial. Before he died he whispered to his wife, Aunt Lucy, "Please, promise me you'll always respect the one percent."

Since then, in honor of Uncle Charlie, we've refused to pay money for any films featuring Latino roles portrayed by non-Latino actors. From Charlton Heston in *A Touch of Evil* to Marisa Tomei in *The Perez Family,* we boycott this type of film out of love, *para respeto* for Uncle Charlie. What could be worse than paying to see Madonna, the greatest offender in cultural appropriation, play a Latin American? But my family had apparently long forgotten the promise to Uncle Charlie.

"Madonna's different now," Gina tried to explain. "She's a mother."

"She's always different." I rolled my eyes. "Every year we see just how different she is."

"Don't talk about Madonna that way," Aunt Lydia bit back. "She doesn't even have a mother. She died when she was a little girl. I saw that on *Oprah*. Even Oprah almost started crying."

"Oprah's always crying."

"Don't say that about Oprah. She's a wonderful person, such a good role model. Why, just the other day I saw her trying to talk Spanish with Gloria Estefan and she was actually doing pretty good!"

* * *

So this was how the dialogue went that Christmas—full of allegiances to beloved celebrities as seen on daytime television and MTV.

And that's why I spent Christmas alone. The front door slammed and shook the wreath on the other side. As I heard the three cars pull out of the driveway I thought of Uncle Charlie. And then in honor of the one percent, I turned up the TV, grabbed some green-and-gold wrapping paper, and began to press.

Third Call

"Chavez residence."

"Hello, is Ernie available?"

"You mean Dr. Ernesto Chavez, Ph.D.?"

"Yes, right."

"No, he is on vacation with his family in Mexico. Is there a message?"

"Well, I worked at an event he organized two months ago and—"

"Are you a student? Because Dr. Chavez doesn't take calls from students at his private residence."

"No, I'm not his student. I worked at an event he had at his home."

"The one for the Chicano Karaoke Club last week?"

"No . . ."

"The Cajete Mujer Conference last weekend?"

"No, no, it was over two months ago and it was a luncheon, at his house. I still haven't received my honorarium and he hasn't returned my calls."

"Well, I will definitely forward this call."

"Thank you, I would appreciate that."

Role Model Rule Number 6

Live Better, Work Union

I'd been working full-time at Annie's Art Emporium for almost a year, selling overpriced brushes to part-time art students and Styrofoam balls to frantic mothers who hissed at their children, "This is NO way to make a solar system, not last minute like this! You need to plan ahead! Next time, you're on your own!" The following week I'd see the same mothers hissing at the same kids, "This is NO way to make the Mission San Buenaventura! You need to plan ahead! Next time, you're on your own!"

It was already mid-May and my annual review was approaching. I knew it was time to ask for more money, maybe some benefits, and definitely my own locker. I had been sharing one with Gary since I first clocked in. Every morning as I put on my orange corduroy smock and plastic name tag, I started the same rant.

"Gary, you know how much we actually earn a day? I mean, a full day's worth of work? Twenty-eight dollars. Can you believe that, Gary? Twenty-eight lousy dollars for being here all day. And that's *before* taxes. And when are they gonna hire more help? You know, I don't even have time for break anymore. We really need to form some kind of union thing."

"A union?" he asked.

"Yeah, you know my uncle Charlie was an actor and he told me a lot of stuff, that people can form these unions to protect themselves from unfair—"

"Oh, come on," Gary interrupted as he looped the long wide apron strings twice around his waist. "Why you wanna start something? At least on Sunday, we don't have to wear the smock."

"Gary, we're closed on Sunday."

"I know, but still."

One day a woman wearing a gauze dress and that bulky jewelry you learn how to make from *Sunset* magazine came into the store. She had a Florence Henderson haircut; not the style she had during her early *Brady Bunch* years, but later, when she was pushing Pam nonstick cooking spray on TV.

She kept looking at me as I rang up her total. Then she squinted her eyes.

"Are you Indian?" she asked.

"Nope," I answered curtly. I knew the procedure. You had to cut 'em off quick because, if you gave 'em one little pause, one little inch of breath, they'd start talking about their last trip to Taos or Santa Fe or how much they loved turquoise jewelry.

I rang up her total and announced, "One hundred and eighty dollars and forty-five cents."

"You sure look Indian," she said as she pulled out a credit card.

"Well, I'm not." I pressed my lips together tightly and formed a stiff smile. First rule of customer service, always smile.

"Are you sure?"

"What, you don't think I know what I am?"

The woman stepped back.

"I'm so sorry." She placed her hand on her chest. "I didn't mean it like that. Really, I didn't. It's just that a lot of people aren't sure about their ancestry. I mean, I didn't find out I was part Swiss until long after I married."

"Oh, that's okay, really," I answered. Second rule of retail service, the customer is always right. Besides, maybe she was correct and maybe I wasn't sure what I was. I did see *Dances with Wolves* three times and really enjoyed it. Anyway, there was no way I could afford to snap at a customer.

The woman looked at my name tag. Shit, now she was gonna call Charlie and complain that she had some surly counter girl with attitude. Good-bye annual raise! Adios, locker.

I swiped her credit card through and even though it cleared, I told her it had been declined. It was so worth it to see the embarrassed, confused look on her face as she searched in her purse for a checkbook.

"I really should cut the card in half," I told her as I gave the card back to her and pretended to do her a favor. "But I'm sure it's just a mistake with the computer."

The next day Gary told me there was a call for me.

"Is this Michele?" the voice asked.

"Yes."

"I don't know if you remember me. I was in the store yesterday. I have a Florence Henderson haircut, not when she was in the *Brady Bunch,* but rather—"

Okay, so she didn't really say the last part.

"Oh, hi, I remember you," I told her. "How can I help you?"

Third rule of customer service, remain pleasant in all circumstances. Plus maybe she knew I lied about her credit-card validation.*

"Well, see, Michele, I'm an artist."

Yes, like every other customer who comes in here.

". . . and I have a show coming up, actually in five weeks, and I don't know how to ask this—"

"Oh, excuse me," I interrupted her. "But I have to help a customer and I'm all alone at the counter."

"Is there another time I could call?" she asked anxiously. "When do you have a free minute, a break?"

"I, well . . . I don't know. I really have to go."

"I'll call again," she added quickly before hanging up.

But she didn't call again. Instead she came by the store the next day when I happened to be out at lunch.

"Hey, Mitchie," Gary said, waving a business card in front of me. "This woman came by asking for you."

"For me?" I slurped the remains of my Loco Half 'n Half.

"Yeah, some artist lady. Here." He gave me the card.

It said Sheila Emmerson. Scrawled in pen were the words "Please call." Hmmm. What was this plea all about? I stuck the card in my smock pocket and told myself I'd call her before I left work. But before I knew it, it was already five o'clock and Julie was picking me up and we were gonna go to L.A. for the weekend. You know how that is. Then, for some reason, when I woke up Sunday morning at Meno's place, I remembered the woman's card

---

I really don't like to lie and I'm not advocating lying. As an aspiring role model, you really shouldn't lie and should always tell the truth. Lying is bad.

in my smock pocket and decided that I'd call her first thing Monday morning.

But Monday I was put in stock inventory and I guess being away from the counter and from people made me forget. On Wednesday I discovered the card was no longer in my pocket and by Friday, well, it was already the weekend again and all I could think about was what outfits I was gonna wear, which boys were gonna be at the club, and who'd make Meno most jealous.

That afternoon the woman surprised me with a call. I was at the counter sorting pens by color and Gary was nearby counting construction-paper packs.

"Is this Michele?" she asked.

"Oh, yes." I recognized her voice.

"This is Sheila Emmerson. I had talked to you about a week ago. I also left a card for you. Did you ever get it?"

"Oh, yeah, I got it but I lost—I mean, it's been busy today."

"Well, I'm calling because I'm wondering if you're interested in some extra work. You know I mentioned I was having a show in about three months and—"

"An art show?"

"Yes, they're showing my work over at the K. T. Vawter Gallery in L.A. Are you familiar with it?"

"Oh yeah," I lied. "I know it. I'm in L.A. all the time."

"Well, since I met you the other day, I really think you can help me."

Great. What does she need? Did she want me to take coats? Serve scones or crossants? I thought I better find out exactly what she needed for her event (see Role Model Rule Number 1).

"Yeah, so what is it that you need, exactly?" I asked. I held the phone between my chin and my shoulder while I rang up another customer.

"Well, I always feel a little awkward just coming out and asking people I don't know, especially if they're not with an agency or anything. Or are you with an agency?"

An agency? Oh, so she did need service help.

"No, I'm not with any agency."

"Oh, so as I mentioned, I'm an artist."

"Yes, you told me that."

"And I think, I think you'd be perfect."

"For what?"

"To model for me."

"You want *me* to model?"

Gary looked up at me. I turned away and cupped the mouthpiece with my hand. The last thing I wanted was him thinking that I thought I could be a model.

"What do you want me to model? Like clothes?"

"No no no." The woman laughed. "I do portraits, figuratives. I really could use you for this next show."

"I don't know." I hesitated. "What do I have to do?"

"Not much really. Just sit still."

"Sit still? For how long?"

"Well, sometimes for a long time."

"What if I have to go to the bathroom?"

"Well, if you have to go, I really think you should go." She laughed again. "I mean, you can take breaks."

"Well, I don't know . . ."

"Of course I'll pay you," she added quickly. "How does ten sound?"

"Ten . . . bucks?"

"Yes."

"For how long?"

"Probably two afternoons. Both Saturday and Sunday."

"Two afternoons for ten bucks?" I asked her. "I don't know, those are my only days off. Maybe I could do one day."

"No, I would pay ten an hour."

"Ten dollars an hour?!"

"Yes."

Ten dollars an hour? I couldn't believe it. Here at Annie's I made a lousy $3.50 an hour. It would take me at least three hours to make what this woman was offering me in only one. Plus all I had to do was sit around with a wind machine in front of me? She was crazy. She must be an artist. She was rich. She was definitely Swiss. So Swiss and rich to be giving so much money away.

"So, could you come to my studio this weekend?" she asked.

I thought of my weekend plans in L.A. Just half an afternoon sitting still for this woman would let me get those strappy slingbacks I wanted. The open-toe black suede ones. I could even get a pedicure. Hot-pink polish. Mmmm . . . and Meno loved toe cleavage.

"Yeah, I'll be there. Just one more thing."

"Yes?"

"You paying under the table?"

"**What** was that about?" Gary asked as I hung up the phone.

"None of your busy-ness," I told him. Suddenly I felt great. Suddenly I felt six feet tall and that every customer in the store viewed me in a new celebrity status. I yawned a fake yawn and stretched my arms across the counter. Suddenly I was bored sorting pens. Suddenly I had attitude. Suddenly I felt just like . . . a supermodel!

I left the counter to go to the employees' bathroom. I was anxious to reevaluate my newly discovered model good looks in a full-length mirror. But once in front of it . . . oh, come on. No way. No fucking way. I stood sideways and sucked in my gut. The bright white-green light exposed pink blemishes on my chin, blackheads on the sides of my nose, and rough skin across my forehead. Were my eyelids always so puffy? Is that a mustache or bad bathroom lighting? Why didn't I get braces while I was still living at home, rent-free and a beneficiary on Mom's dental plan?

I went to the stockroom and used the phone. I called the woman back.

"Oh, hi, Michele," she answered. Then she sounded nervous. "Oh, please don't tell me you need to cancel."

"No, it's not that," I assured her. "It's just I wanted to know why you asked me to model. I mean, I'm not really model material." Just saying the words hit my ego hard.

"Well, I pick people for different reasons," she said. "A certain look, a particular feature. One of the first things that really attracted me to you was your nose."

"My nose?"

"Yeah, it's not one of those typical small, little, upturned things. You know everyone and their mother has a nose like that, or I should say, everyone who reads *Marie Claire* and then goes out to get a nose job. Your nose looks very—how should I say?— Indian?"

"Indian?"

"Yes. Is there a problem with that?"

I slowly squeezed the sides of my nose and thought about her question. Well, yes, there was a problem with that. This woman was totally exoticizing me. It was plain and simple. I read about this type of behavior, this particular form of racism in that book *Making Face, Making Soul* and actually in an episode of *What's Happening!* when Shirley is hired for a job 'cause she made the work environment more "interesting." Last thing I wanted was to be some exploited subject and be put on display for this woman's little art show. Yes, there was definitely a problem. But how do I go about making my point? Writing a poem about it was out of the question (see Role Model Rule Number 1). What could I say or do to make it clear to people like her that they can't always get what they want? God, it was so uncomfortable. Then Uncle Charlie came to mind.

"I didn't know it was my nose you wanted."

"What do you mean?"

"I'm afraid . . . well . . ." I cringed. "You can't have it for less than . . . two hundred dollars."

"Two hundred dollars!"

"A day."

"That's a lot just for a nose."

"Yes, but it's an Indian-looking nose, a member of . . ."

"Of?"

"The local union, Union 233." My home address, but she wouldn't know. "Aren't you familiar with it?"

"Uh, yes," she said. I could tell she was lying. "But my show," she started. "It's in five—well, now four weeks and—"

"And I have the nose."

"Yes, you do," she agreed slowly. "And I wouldn't want to break any union rules."

"And I wouldn't want you to."

"Okay, so . . . I guess I'll see you on Saturday."

"Of course."

I hung up the phone and put my hand to my nose. I squeezed the sides of it again. It was Uncle Rudy's nose, Grandpa Rudy's nose, and a little bit of, well, you know the story. And thank God I inherited their nose, 'cause my "particular feature" knew how to sniff out opportunity. This nose would never be caught dead in a *Marie Claire* spread, but was able to negotiate supply and demand. And so my little Indian nose went all the way to the bank after having made four hundred bucks in just two afternoons during the month of May.

Tenth Call

"Hello?"

"Hey, Michele."

"Oh. Hey, Louie."

"Damn, nice to hear you, too!"

"No, it's not that. It's just I thought you were this dude who owes me money. I just left the hundredth message at his office and man, it's like I read at his event over eight months ago and he still hasn't paid me. So, anyway, you wanna talk to Angela?"

"How much does he owe you?"

"Well, it's not that much, but you know, I'm just thinking I'm gonna skip it. It's not worth the bother anymore."

"What? You can't do that!"

"I just hate sounding like a nag."

"*He's* the one making you feel that way. Besides, it's the principle of the thing. I mean, everyone wants their artist to add culture or spice to their event, but they don't wanna acknowledge their worth. You should try being a DJ."

"I couldn't imagine."

"This dude's white?"

"No, brown."

"Oh shit, good luck! They're the worst!"

"Don't say that."

"They always pay their own people last, if at all."

"Oh, that's not true. This guy, he's like Mr. Community and everything. He's just busy and stuff. Really, he's down for brown."

"No, listen. It's not about brown, black, or white, it's all about green."

Breaking the Major Rule

If only Angela would have been home that day. I would have just asked for my sweater, she would have given it to me, and that would have been that. But no, she had to be out shopping. So, in a way, what happened is her fault.

The sweater was the black wool one that I had found in a movie theater. It itched the hell out of my skin the minute I put it on and normally I would have thought of scabies and ditched the thing. But the inside label said Banana Republic and the theater was the Showcase over on La Brea. Fancy brand, nice part of La Brea—rich people don't have scabies. It must be the wool, I thought. So of course I kept the sweater and of course Angela borrowed it all the time 'cause it looked "too cute" with her light baby-blue T.

When I went into Angela's room that day to get it back, her phone rang. Her machine could have taken the message, but for some reason I picked up the receiver. It was some lady from the community center and she said that they were very impressed with Angela's videotape. Would she be available for an audition?

"Oh, of course." I grabbed a purple spiral notebook off the floor. "Angela's talked so much about your play. When are auditions?"

The woman gave me all the information and then stressed, "We're really behind schedule, so if she's interested, she must call us back today. We're casting parts quickly."

I wrote down the message on the first blank page of the notebook. Oooh, Angela was gonna be so excited about this and I was gonna be the one to make her day! I couldn't wait for her to come home from shopping.

I hung up the phone, tore the sheet out of the spiral, and happened to notice some writing on the second page. It was in Angela's handwriting and a date was written on the upper right-hand corner. When I flipped to the next page another date was written on that upper right-hand corner. It was then I realized what I was holding wasn't just a mere spiral notebook, but Angela's diary. I quickly shut it, put the message on the foot of her bed, and threw my sweater in the basket that was parked in the hallway. I thought nothing else about the whole thing—the phone call, the spiral, her borrowing my sweater for the nth time and stinking it up with CK One, but as I walked down the stairs to the garage, there was one thing I couldn't get out of my mind—was that *my* name in her notebook?

I went into the garage, put the basket on top of the dryer, and turned the washing machine on. Was that really my name? And if it was, what could she have possibly said about me? Nothing bad, right? I mean, I know I'm a pretty nice person and I'm not just a good roommate but a great friend. I was sure what she wrote about me was good. I mean, Angela loved me. It was evident in the way she did things for me, not just as a roommate, but as a friend. How she lies to Mark W. when I'm out with Doze and how she hides all those little encouraging Post-it-notes in my Dayrunner. What about Dia de la Rocha—the day she took me to see Rage Against the Machine at Irvine Meadows just to celebrate our one-year anniversary as roommates? Did I mention I was a great friend?

I threw the sweater into the wash and watched it get sucked in slowly by the whirlpool of cold water. I shut the lid and walked up the stairs back to our apartment. The thought of my name in her diary nagged at me. Maybe it wasn't my name. Maybe it was Michael. Maybe it said Ma Chérie. Maybe Angela was practicing her French. Maybe she had a girl on the side. Maybe.

I walked back into the apartment and into her bedroom. I opened the spiral to that first page. There it was, my name. Not Michael, not French, no lesbian love triangle—just my name like I saw earlier. M-i-c-h-e-l-e. I tossed the spiral back on the carpet and left her room. I mean, that's all I really wanted to know. I went back down the stairs and into the garage. I had forgotten to put soap in the wash.

I had just broken the major rule—you do not read other people's private journals. You just don't do it. It's like one of those things you learn early in life or remember from an episode of *The Waltons.* But I didn't really read her diary, per se, I just wanted to make sure it was my name. That's all I wanted to know. Just one word, seven little letters. It wasn't as though I read anything else. Just my own name, and she doesn't own that, does she? She doesn't own *me.* But if only I hadn't noticed the other words surrounding it: Sometimes. Can. Be. So. *"Sometimes Michele can be so . . ."* That's the exact sentence Angela wrote on the last line of the page.

So, *what?* I measured a quarter cup of soap. So, so . . . clean? I evened out the amount. So precise? I gently shook the cup and leveled the soap more. So anal? Nah, that wasn't it. I threw the soap in and slammed the lid shut. Sometimes I can be so aggres-

sive with my applied laundry procedures? I went up the stairs
back into the apartment. Okay, so whatever I was, I was that way
only some of the time. And this "something" I supposedly was,
was definitely a negative. I mean, people don't say someone "can
be so . . ." when it's a positive thing. You never hear, "Sometimes
Missy can be so nice." You're more likely to hear "Sometimes
Missy can be such a super-precise anal-retentive bitch." Did Angela think that about me? When have I been a bitch to Angela?
Not recently. I mean, it could have been a bad day, this day I was
supposedly such a bitch. Maybe I snapped at her or something.
Maybe I was just tired that day. I mean excuse me, but between
work and school, and Mark W. and Doze, a girl can get tired.
God, Angela, give me a fucking break! It was probably just a day
I was tired. Can't I be allowed just one single day when I don't
have to be "on"? But what day was it?

I went back into Angela's room and opened the spiral again.
The top of the page that mentioned my name was dated May 28.
May 28? What was May 28? What was . . . May . . . oh yeah, that
was the day, the night I had a reading with Pura Cultura. That was
the night Angela showed up with Louie to hear me read new work.
Oh, it was so obvious that she and Louie were in a bad mood. I
mean, it was totally them. They were all late and didn't say anything after I was done reading, and Angela really didn't mix with
anyone. I mean, she and Louie just left as soon as the reading was
over with. I even specifically asked her later what she thought of
my new stories and she just answered nonchalantly, "Oh, they
were fine." But what did she really mean by that? Sometimes she
can say one thing and mean something entirely different. That's
not very direct. Not very honest, is it? Maybe she thought my new
stories were lousy. Maybe she thought *I* was lousy. Maybe someone like her really can't give an honest critique to someone like
me, an *artist,* who most definitely needs feedback in order to pro-

duce quality work. Fuck! Everybody knows that the positive evo-
lution of any artist depends on honest criticism. It was obvious I
had to read the rest of her diary entry, for the sake of *art.*

I turned the page and discovered to my horror, the top of the
back page was blank. Her sentence about me was not finished! A
brand-new entry started in the middle of the page and it looked—
and I'm just guessing 'cause I didn't read it—like it was about
her and Louie's weekend trip to San Diego. Talk about a short
attention span! I shut the spiral and left her room.

I went to the living room and turned on the TV. You know,
what did Angela know about poetry or literature or art for that
matter anyway? I mean, it's not like she's the most well-read
person in the world. Who was *she* to judge *me*? Me, who actually
won an award for poetry in the sixth grade. Me, who actually
knew it was a Robert Frost poem used in *The Outsiders* way before
I even read the credits, thank you. Who the hell was Angela?
With her little spiral, writing down her stupid little thoughts, in
her dingy little room, in MY sweater?

Just then I heard a key in the front door.

"Hey, you!" It was Angela.

She put her bag on the coffee table (now a real one, not made
from boxes of books and covered with batik fabric) and pulled out
two scrunchies. They were black cloth woven with thick silver
ribbon. "Look, they had these on sale and I instantly thought of
you. They'll show up in your hair real cute." She tossed one to
me. I didn't reach out to get it but rather let it land on the floor
near my leg.

"What's wrong?" she asked.

"Nothing." I looked at the TV. "I'm just tired." *Tired, not bitchy.*

Angela made a face and went into her room. "Shit!" I heard
her say. "No messages?"

I thought of the sheet of paper I'd left for her. She would see it any minute and to be honest, part of me didn't want her to have it. Why was she deserving of information, when she herself couldn't even share information with me? Why should I help out with her little career when it was obvious she wasn't interested in helping mine? I got up from the couch and walked down the hallway to her door. It was open and I saw her sitting on the edge of her bed, going through the rest of her shopping bag. The spiral was still on the floor and I saw that the sheet of paper was still on the foot of her bed. I knew I could easily go in and grab it. She wasn't even paying attention. And if she did notice, I'd just say it was the new chore list I accidentally left in her room when I went in to get the sweater. My sweater. She'd never even know.

"Can I come in?" I asked.

"Sure." Angela didn't look up. "You don't have to ask."

I looked at the spiral. I knew inside were Angela's personal thoughts, opinions, and innermost secrets. I knew she felt comfortable leaving it around her room like that, 'cause after all, her roommate was a writer and I, more than anyone, would respect what someone puts on paper—words that can be written in the heat of passion, words that can be easily taken out of context by a second reader, or incorrectly interpreted by a third party. Keeping a journal is one of the most courageous acts a person, a *woman,* can do. It documents and validates, gives an outlet to dialogue we normally may not feel comfortable ever voicing. It allows us an opportunity to express that inner hesitation that challenges us every waking day. You should never judge anyone for what they write in a diary.

I walked toward the edge of the bed and took the sheet of paper. I was right—Angela didn't even look up. She wasn't even paying attention. Maybe she wasn't paying attention when I read the new stories on May 28. Or was she? Hmmm. I clenched the paper in my hand. I knew exactly what I should do with it.

Sometimes I can be so . . .

Buy American

It was my third upset stomach that month. I found stomachaches easier to fake 'cause the last time I claimed I had a cold, the congested sound in my voice fluctuated and my sincerity was instantly questioned. Before that, I had a migraine and two weeks before that, I had food poisoning from some nasty ol' seafood salad I supposedly ate in Mar Vista.

"Where have you been eating?" my aunt Tura asked again. "My God, you're too young to be having so many problems."

Whenever my family called, it was more acceptable to claim health problems than to admit that I was merely writing and that being the sole reason I couldn't talk with them. Why would I rather want to edit an essay than hear how adorable KaKooey, Grandma Sally's rottweiler, looked sleeping in an old refrigerator box outside? Why would I choose revising a commentary over discovering how many avocados Great-grandpa Louie found rotting under his tree? ("Ay, it's gonna be a bad year for guacamole!")

Yes, to my family, writing was not important. Writing was somewhat selfish. Writing was just plain rude.

Therefore, sickness became an integral part of my professional writing career. Sickness was something my family understood. An indisposition they could sympathize with. Taking care of oneself when ill was very important, 'cause if you didn't, you could get a relapse and miss lots of work or worse, you could die and miss lots and lots of work. Being Mexican, I grew up to understand that missing work is bad. Very bad. A Mexican without a strong work ethic? *Come on.*

So, when Tura called I claimed that I had a major upset stomach and that I really couldn't talk 'cause, well, I was just in too much pain. But really, I was sitting in front of the computer staring at a blank screen, waiting and waiting for a story to come to me. My friend José Jones publishes a local zine and he said if I had a story to him by the weekend he'd consider publishing it. He might even take me to Tito's as payment. I couldn't imagine giving up free tacos at Tito's (see Role Model Rule Number 1).

So there I was hoping it would be just a matter of time before some intense concentration would spark an explosion of creativity. The last thing I needed was some chatty tía or chismosa cousin to call, but when the phone rang, there I had to go and answer it. And wouldn't you know it? It was Tura, Aunt Tura—the worst of all repeat offenders. No matter how many times you repeat you gotta get off the phone, she just keeps yakking and yakking.

"So I really can't talk," I told her. "I wanna make sure I get better today so I don't miss work tomorrow."

"So, what have you been eating?" she questioned me again.

"Well, last night I had four tri tip tacos . . . you know, left over from Alma's . . ." My voice started to trail off.

"You're always with the stomach problems." She clicked her tongue.

"Yeah, I guess so." I rolled my eyes then looked at my blank computer screen. God, couldn't she take a hint?

"Maybe you inherited this from your auntie Chaya," she continued. "You know, she always had the stomach pains."

Great. Here we go with another story about some ancient aunt who I had never heard of, never met, but of course shared her exact same medical condition. It was my clue to tune out.

"I didn't know her," I told Tura curtly. "So anyway, I'm just gonna rest and wait for my Pepto-Bismol to kick in."

"Yeah, Chaya had the stomach problems," Tura went on. "But they were actually ulcers and that's a little different from what you have, huh? But they were all because of that Bug she used to have. Do you ever hear about that VW Bug she used to have?"

"Nuh-uh." Christ. How could I've known about someone's car if I had never heard of them? And hadn't Tura heard what I just said? I was sick. Sick. Should I just hang up and pretend we got disconnected? Nah, 'cause then she'd think I passed out or something and then she'd call 911, or worse she'd drive over herself and then I'd never get any writing done. God, I hated family stories and here I was about to endure another one.

"That VW was the cutest car," Aunt Tura remarked. "You'd be driving down Saviers and everyone would just look at you in that thing. It was like one of those little toy cars you'd drive at Disneyland or something. But it gave her so many problems."

I could've put her on hold. Would she even notice? What about speakerphone? That'd be sort of funny plus her voice would be muffled enough so I wouldn't really have to pay attention to what she was saying. Oh, why not? She wouldn't even know the difference. I pushed the speaker button on, put the phone back on its cradle, and got up to get more butter for my ham sandwich.

"So many problems with that car," I could hear Aunt Tura's

voice echo down the hallway. "Not car problems, like the engine or the windshield blades not working, if you know what I mean."

"Uh-huh," I answered from the kitchen, and she didn't even notice.

"But problems because of all the attention she'd get. You know what I mean?"

"Nuh-uh." I answered as I reentered my room. I opened my filing cabinet and pulled out a manila folder filled with newspaper articles I had once found interesting. Maybe one of them would spark something.

"Well, there'd she'd be coming out of B&D or Bob's," Tura continued. "And there was always some man admiring the VW's back motor or the tires, what are those called with the white around them? White walls?"

"Uh-huh." I started to read a newspaper clipping about a two-hundred-pound thirteen-year-old in Tennessee stuck in his tree house. TENNESSEE TEEN TUBBY IN A TIGHT SQUEEZE, the headline read.

"Well, between you and I, I think men just made up more questions about the car just to keep talking to Chaya, and you know she was so beautiful back then. A regular Latin Rita Hayworth."

"Rita Hayworth *was* Latina."

"She is? I mean, she was? Well, anyway, Chaya just answered what questions she could about the car, but you know Oxnard. Everyone knows each other and it got back to Uva, her third husband, that his wife was talking to strange men in parking lots."

"Uva? That's a weird name."

"Yeah, he was German, just like their car. Funny, huh? Chaya was always with the foreigners and the foreign cars. She never bought American."

"Uh-huh." I read that the tree-house teen was stuck for six

days. I started highlighting quotes from his neighbors. *"Well, they're here talking 'bout chopping down the tree and I just don't know about that. That there tree is ancient, planted right in by the founders of our city. I mean, I know we're here talking about a human life, but what about the tree?"*

"Uva would get jealous and they would have these horrible fights and he threatened that if he heard one more story, just *one more* story about her flirting with strange men, that he was gonna take away her car keys and he was gonna drive her whenever she needed to go somewhere. Can you image? A grown woman having to rely on a man to drive her around?"

"Nuh-uh."

"So anyway, whenever Chaya drove the car to B&D or to Bob's, she just prayed no man would be waiting by it when she came out. And of course, this made her so nervous and tense. Wouldn't it make you tense?"

"Uh-huh." The Tennessee tubby story was just too sad and I guess it wasn't really "me" enough. I crumpled the article up and tossed it into the wastebasket. I found another clipping about Dinky, the Taco Bell Chihuahua. Irate Mexican entertainment types were upset upon learning that Dinky's voice was dubbed not by a Mexican, but by an Argentinean! I highlighted more quotes. *"Sure the actor doing the voice-over is Latino, but when does a Mexican actor get his opportunity to portray a Mexican lead?"*

"Well, actually, this 'Mexican lead' originated from China. Chihua-huas were first bred in China."

"See what I mean? Another blow to la raza!"

"All the time she'd drive that VW clutching her side," Aunt Tura continued. "And finally one day, when she pulled up in her own driveway, there was another car blocking her space. And can you guess whose car it was?"

"Nuh-uh." I logged onto the Internet. There was a story about teen gangs in the heartland. Hmmm . . . could I possibly turn that into something Chicano lit–like?

"The car belonged to Margie Luna," Tura said. "You know, Julia's daughter? She was coming out of the side gate, out of the backyard right when Chaya was pulling up."

"Uh-huh."

"Now, Margie didn't have a cute little VW. She had a Ford. An American car."

"Uh-huh." God, what was the fucking point of this story?

"Oh well, as I was saying, she asked why Chaya was holding the side of her stomach and Chaya said it was nothing. But that Margie tells her she's gonna go to the store to get her a bicarbonate and asked if Chaya wanted to go with her and can you guess what happened?"

"Nuh-uh." Hanging up on Tura began to sound better and better each second she babbled on.

"Well, Margie got behind the steering wheel and Chaya got in the passenger seat and Margie drove 'em over toward Bob's Market and wouldn't you know it?"

"What?" I took a bite of my sandwich.

"They never returned."

"Never returned what?"

"No, I mean, Chaya and Margie never returned. They were both never seen again!"

"Wait, she just took off with Margie?"

"Uh-huh."

"Tura." I pushed myself away from the computer and picked up the phone receiver. "You mean this Auntie Chaya left her husband, left Oxnard, left with the clothes on her back with another woman and was never seen again?"

"Uh-huh."

"Wait, what did Uva say?" I badgered her for answers. "How'd he react?"

"Well," Tura answered slowly, "we later discovered that she wasn't even married to Uva."

"What?"

"He was really just a contact for Chaya. She used him to sell things, like Styrofoam tortilla warmers and stuff, to German boutiques. You know the Germans, they really like Mexican things and she had a pretty good little business."

"Are you serious?"

"And that day she took off with Margie she drained her whole account," Tura added. "Must of been in the high hundred thousands, at least! I heard they're living in Stuttgart. That's in Germany."

"Tura." I opened a new file on my computer. "This is a crazy story!"

Suddenly I heard a click.

"Tura, you still there?" I asked.

"Oh, I better go," she said. "You know, it's probably Emma on the other line."

"No, Tura, wait."

"No, I better take her call. She never takes no for an answer and I can never get her off the phone."

"Wait! Tura, just tell me one thing."

The phone clicked again.

"Sorry, Cheli," she interrupted. "I hate to be rude, but I gotta take this call."

"Wait," I begged for more time. "How come I never heard this story before? How come no one in the family has ever brought this up before?"

"What do you mean, 'brought this up before'? We always talk about Chaya. You just never paid attention."

"No, Tura, I swear. I've never heard this story."

"You know." She sighed heavily. "You really are a lot like Chaya."

"You mean with my stomachaches?"

"No," she said slowly. "In the way that what Chaya wanted, what she really needed, was in her own backyard, and with you, well, I think you don't bother to look in your own backyard."

"My own backyard?" I looked at my blank computer screen. I glanced at my newspaper clippings. "Tura, what do you mean?"

"Mi'ja," Tura said quickly before clicking over to Aunt Emma, "if you want a real story, you need to look in your backyard more often."

Let's go Mexico!

Part of it was 'cause I wanted to read Olga's poems the way she wanted them read, not some translation by a Ph.D. and I also thought it'd be cool too if I knew what Beck was saying when he sings in Spanish. But the real reason I wanted to learn Spanish was so I could talk behind white people's backs.

These are minor explanations, but the main reason I wanted to learn more Spanish was for credit. The foreign-language credit. I couldn't graduate without it.

"You don't speak Spanish?" my counselor asked, surprised.

"Not really," I told her. "I mean, I could improve."

"Well, I don't know what to say," she said, looking over my transcripts. "I don't see how you're going to get the credit you need and still graduate in June. You're going to have to stay here at least another year."

It was late summer and I was going over my class selections with her. For the past months all I could think about was my final summer as a student and here she was telling me that I had another year of classes? No way. I'd been at Santa Monica College off and on for six fucking years and now the supposedly simple two-year stint at UCLA was gonna take me longer? Nuh-uh. *No way.*

"What if I switch majors?" I asked desperately.

"Not at this point," she answered matter-of-factly. She pulled a slim catalog off her office shelf. "You could go on a study abroad program. That way you'll get the credit in a matter of months rather than taking three quarters here. What about Mexico? You've been to Mexico, right?"

I immediately thought of my weekends with Mark W. Mark W. was a typical blond surfer boy who really did say "dude" all the time and, just like me, was sometimes a student. We often extended weekend jaunts to a five full days down in Ensenada. During the afternoons we packed the trunk of his Subaru with Kahlua and firecrackers. And in the evenings, oh man, the evenings we filled twenty-buck hotel rooms with the smell of our sexy funk. Of course I'd been to Mexico. But then I remembered CeCe, who said Baja doesn't really count as Mexico.

"No," I told my counselor, "I haven't been to Mexico, really."

"So, you've never *really* been to Mexico and you *really* don't speak Spanish," she said. "Well, do you *really* want to graduate?"

I picked Taxco as the place to learn—I mean, *improve* my Spanish. Located ninety miles southwest of Mexico City, it's a charming silver mining town clinging to the steep hills of Guerrero state. Locals, eager to practice their English with visiting American students, make it an ideal setting for the total Spanish immersion experience. I got that part out of the catalog. You don't think I really talk like that, do you? In the catalog there were pictures of students (white) lounging around the school's swimming pool (aqua blue) being served piña coladas by waiters (brown). Another photo had two female students (white) buying jewelry (silver) from native artisans (brown). I looked at the photos and wondered how I'd fit in.

The whole application process seemed simple enough. You filled out an application, wrote an essay of intent, and sat for an informal interview to prove you could speak enough Spanish to get you through customs. While I was waiting in line for my interview, I met two other students (white) who were gonna go to Taxco as well. When I overhead their own interviews before me, I grew nervous. Their Spanish was so good! When it was my turn, all I could think about was how well the other two students had spoken. Finally, after an excruciating ten-minute conversation en español, the two interviewers (white) smiled and said, "Have a great time in Taxco!" Whew!

After my departure date was set, I arranged for the time off work, sublet my room to a friend, bought a fanny pack (yeah, right), and promised my man I wouldn't fool around with anyone south of either border. By late January, when everyone would be searching for sweaters off the Gap sale rack, I'd be in sunny Mexico, speaking Spanish, sipping margaritas, and preparing to graduate, on time, in June.

We took a minibus into Taxco. There were three buses, all filled with students from other parts of the country who'd picked Mexico as the place to study Spanish. As soon as we drove under the main road's archway and entered the town of Taxco, I immediately sensed the whole population was familiar with minibuses such as ours. The locals actually waved us in.

Once all the students and coordinators arrived at the school, there was a welcome luncheon in our honor. We were served apricot-marinated quail in roasted chipotle sauce and corn pudding on a veranda overlooking a swimming pool that was filled with brown water and tadpoles. A Scottish student asked me, "Is this how you ate at home, growing up?"

"Oh yeah," I bragged, thinking of the Hamburger Helper, Spanish Style, my mom whipped up on payday Fridays. After lunch all of us heaved our luggage to the school's main entrance and waited to be picked up by our *caseras*, new host families. One student, Kevin, his casero was this long-haired dude who pulled up in a black late-model Jeep. The casero was wearing tight faded jeans and a belt buckle in the shape of a mota leaf.

Funny, some Spanish comes naturally.

"Sweet!" Kevin exclaimed as he picked up his backpack and flung it in the Jeep's backseat. Then the two drove off, leaving us in a trail of dust behind them. Sounds clichéd, but it really did happen that way.

Twelve more students were picked up by their new caseras and then there were five of us left, standing around talking. About ten minutes later, a white VW Bug made its way up the hill. It stalled halfway and we all waited for it to start up again, but we could hear the engine trying to turn over. It wasn't gonna move.

The driver got out and lifted the hood of the Bug while a woman in the backseat got out and walked up the hill toward us.

"Shit, I hope she's not here for me," I overheard someone remark. "I don't wanna be stuck with a family without a car."

"That's not her car, stupid. It's a taxi."

"A VW taxi? Don't Mexicans know they catch on fire?"

The woman spoke to our program coordinator and then he looked at his clipboard and called out my name. The woman was here for me. I looked over at her and she smiled. The coordinator then called out four more additional names.

"Wait," I told him before walking over to the woman. "I didn't ask for roommates. I requested a private residence, my own room."

Even though I was speaking English, his native language, he acted like he didn't understand.

"We'll work on the details later." He patted me on the back. "Just go for now. Go with the flow." He looked back at his clipboard quickly.

My number of housemates doubled in a matter of a week. A friend told one friend and then they told one friend and so on and so on. It got around how grand our house was: a three-story home with a spacious sun deck, laundry facilities (muy importante), strong water pressure (más importante), and a lush courtyard. All for about a hundred bucks a month. There was always unfamiliar luggage curbed near the front door ready to be unpacked, and Señora Saldana, my new casera, was always eager to take the extra renters and the extra cash. Out of all the household amenities, I think everyone dug the lush courtyard the most. It allowed students to brag in postcards to home, "Dear Nathan, as I write this, I'm relaxing in a sunny authentic Mexican courtyard. I feel quite festive surrounded by all the clay pottery and native foliage."

My first housemates were white girls. In their white socks and fancy sneaks, they shared stories of summers spent in Spain and how Mexico was so different. I called the girls I lived with the White Socks and labeled them differently by appearance or character traits. There was Dandruff Sock, Pink Sock, Clinique Sock, PMS Sock, and Slutty Sock.

While the White Socks marveled at the quaintness of Mexican culture, I could only feel so fairly familiar with it. From waking up to roosters crowing each dawn to keeping tabs on the amount of manteca left in its red box in the fridge, this was what I was used to in my childhood home in Oxnard. But then again, I never had no White Sock in my house correcting my Spanish.

"No, Michele, it's *el* problema, not *la* problema," Clinique Sock reprimanded me. "Wanna know a little secret? Think of a problem as a man. Men are always problems, right? If 'problem' is masculine, that means its equivalent article is masculine as well. So it would be the masculine *el* rather than the feminine *la*. Get it?"

But the White Socks didn't think the men in Mexico were such problems. They embraced every brown boy who clicked his tongue at them.

"Damn, they're so horny," Slutty Sock complained loudly in class as she checked her neck for hickeys with Clinique Sock's compact mirror. "I've gotta make sure I keep track of my pill, 'cause these men are just so into making babies and starting families and I ain't gonna be no green card for no one. That's the last thing I wanna do. I got career goals. That's why I'm even here in the fucking first place. Being bilingual is only gonna advance my opportunities in the workforce."

One night the White Socks wanted me to go out with them.

"My God, you're such a homebody," Pink Sock remarked. "You're gonna get old before your time."

I was old. Actually the oldest of anyone in the whole program. But they didn't know that. I had shaved five years off my age and told my roommates I was only twenty-two. To be Chicana and not speak Spanish well was one thing, but to be counting twenty-eight candles on my next birthday cake and still an undergrad? Forget it. I couldn't bear a double dose of jabs, no matter how playfully intended. Yes, sometimes I can be so fragile, like a flower. Or like Selena sang, "como la flor." In Spanish, flowers are feminine.

"Becky's right," Dandruff Sock agreed. "You oughta come out with us. We got the Macarena down and Lido's cousin from Mexico City is coming down. I'm sure we could find you someone who speaks slow. What are you gonna do? Stay here and watch novelas with Mati all night?"

They all laughed and two of them did a high five. I felt a sudden chill.

Truth was I wanted to hang out with Mati. She was Señora Saldana's helper (not *maid*) and the one who picked us up from the school that day. She was about four feet eleven with long thin black hair she kept back in two faded gold bobby pins, and she had these bulging calves from running daily errands on the steep streets of Taxco. At nineteen, she was just about the youngest of all of us, but looked the most hardened. When she didn't spend Saturday nights in her scuffed white pumps and red velveteen dress down at the zócalo, she could be found in the kitchen watching the lineup of Mexican soaps on a mini black-and-white TV and frying up tortillas in some form of a snack. I couldn't think of a more enjoyable evening.

"Nah," I told the White Socks. "I'm just gonna catch up on my studying."

After the White Socks bailed, I went into the kitchen to hang out with Mati. She heated up a piece of lard the size of a Rubik Cube in the frying pan while I turned up the volume on the opening credits of *Marisol*. Everyone knows the best part is when Enrique sings the title song.

"That Enrique sure is fine," I told her in Spanish. "More than his father. I just love that mole!"

"Oh, yes," she agreed in English. "The mole!"

Wow. Sex *is* the universal language.

The next morning PMS Sock told me, "You know, Michele, if you really want to make the most of Mexico, you're gonna have to make more of an effort to get involved with its people. You wouldn't believe all the people we met last night and here you stayed cooped up with Mati watching TV."

"I heard you made tostadas," Pink Sock piped in as she picked the peeling skin off her nose.

"Yeah, we did."

"You did?" Dandruff Sock asked. "Hey, did Mati show you how to get the tortilla in the shape of a bowl like at El Torito? How do they do that anyway?"

It was only a matter of weeks before I grew homesick. Really homesick. I began to feel isolated not having anyone to have a real conversation with. Why hadn't I taken CeCe's advice and borrowed her Walkman?

"No no no," I had told her. "I don't want any major modern conveniences from home. I wanna fully embrace Mexican culture in its natural setting. I wanna inhale the language, the music, the people." But by the third week, I was jonesing for a *People* magazine (not "en español") and a Carl's Jr. Famous Star with no onion didn't sound bad at all.

I was out on the patio when I heard a commercial break through the static on Mati's kitchen radio. A familiar jingle *en inglés* hit me hard. Oh, that little jingle brought back so many memories, so much nostalgia, and so many thoughts of *home*. Before I knew it, the jingle was over and I was left cruelly unsatisfied. I realized if I wanted to get over being homesick, I would have to travel to Cuernavaca, the town tagged "Eternal Springtime." I decided to travel there the following Sunday morning and by Saturday evening everyone knew of my plans.

"Oh, I heard you're going into Cuernavaca," Pink Sock said. "You gonna eat at Las Mañanitas? I read they have the best Swisschard tamales there. At least that's what I read in *Let's Go Mexico*."

"Oh, then I'm sure it's true."

"Hey, can you make a trip to the mercado for me?" PMS Sock asked. "I hear they have every kind of herb and root under the sun there. Maybe there's something that could help with my cramps."

"Don't forget to visit Museo Robert Brady," Clinique Sock added as she applied Turn-Around cream to her face. "He was a white man who was really into Mexican stuff."

"Really?"

"I hear the guys are fine in Cuernavaca," Slutty Sock said, looking at herself in the bedroom mirror. "Maybe I should go with you."

"Well, I sorta wanna go on my own."

"Hey, you should go with someone. Cuernavaca is like an hour away," Clinique Sock said. "I mean, in *Let's Go Mexico*, it says women in Mexico really shouldn't travel alone."

"Well, maybe tourist-looking women," I said. "But I mean, I think I can blend in."

"Yeah, until you open your mouth!" PMS Sock laughed. Then all five White Socks high-fived and I suddenly felt that chill again.

The next morning I woke up at six A.M. The White Socks were snoring off tequila shots in their rooms. Mati was the only one awake in the whole house. She was in the kitchen, separating cloves of garlic and dividing them for the upcoming week.

"Vas a Cuernavaca?" she asked.

"Yeah," I told her.

She frowned.

"Sí," I corrected myself.

I decided to wear baggy jeans, an oversized flannel, and my cash in my bra. Yeah, Cuernavaca was only an hour away, but if

Let's Go Mexico said women should be careful traveling alone, I wouldn't take any chances.

Once I arrived at Cuernavaca's main bus station, I walked into La Plaza de Armas, the city's square, and strolled past the mercado, and definitely past Las Mañanitas. When I came across some ATMs and a gas station, I could almost feel I was getting closer to what I was looking for. I asked a few people for directions and they pointed up to a street and told me to turn on a street called Vía San Robles. One block later and before I knew it, what I had been looking for was smack in front of me. I looked up, covered my mouth in excitement, and hurried in.

I took a seat at the Formica counter and looked around. Oh, just the interior design, from the color schemes on the walls to the textured vinyl of the stools, took me back home to, dare I say it, "el otro lado." The aroma from the kitchen, even the piped in Muzak, made me think of all the Sunday mornings, the weekends I spent surrounded by—double-dare me to say it—*Mexican-American* memories.

Finally a woman in a blue dress and white apron came up to me and asked, "Café?"

I nodded. She poured me some coffee, then asked, "Lista?"

Of course I was ready. I had been ready all week and I knew exactly what my heart and appetite had been aching for. The homesick pangs had grown stronger and more intense as each day in Taxco passed.

But when she asked to take my order I paused. Oh, my God, had I already forgotten? I suddenly went blank. I felt light-headed, somewhat dizzy. I focused on the picture place card on my table and what I had come for quickly came back to me.

"Yes," I told her. "I'll have—I mean, quiero un Rooty Tooty Fresh 'n Fruity."

"Jamón o salchicha?"

"Salchicha."

"Un Rooty Tooty Fresh y Fruity con salchicha!" she yelled to the cook.

I took a sip of my coffee. I saw the same cook pour small puddles of pancake batter onto the greased-up griddle and lay some sausage next to it.

That Sunday morning, all my loneliness was lifted.

It was on a Monday that Eva came to class. New students always started classes on Monday and she showed up on CP Time* wearing a Blondie-tour T-shirt and flip-flops. She had green eyes, dyed black hair, and the skin color people call olive. Was she or wasn't she? I thought to myself from the back of the room as she took an empty seat near the door. She did have that look. It would be so wonderful to have a friend. During lunch, I just came right out and asked her The Question. (see Role Model Rule Number 8).

"So, where you from?"

"Arizona," she told me. "Mesa, to be exact, but my dad's side's from Mexico. My mom, she's from El Salvador."

"So they didn't speak Spanish at home?"

"No way. They already had so much discrimination and shit, they didn't want their kids going through that. They just wanted us to speak English, all the time."

She looked over at the White Socks. "I hate those girls."

---

*Chicano People Time; sometimes called Colored People Time—meaning late, tardy. Chris Rock says the only thing the white man's got over us is that he's on time and I couldn't agree more. Even if you're not an aspiring role model, you should make every effort to be on time for everything. When you're late, you make us all look bad.

Here was finally someone who shared my sentiment, yet surprisingly I found myself saying, "Oh, they're not so bad. Pink Sock—I mean, Becky, is okay. In small doses."

"Those are the kind of girls," Eva continued as she took a bite of her torta, "that kept me from speaking Spanish."

"What do you mean?"

"I mean, those girls," she continued looking at them, "are the type that made fun of anyone who didn't look like them, dress like them, or talk like them. So finally in high school, when I wanted to learn Spanish, there was no way I wanted to sound Mexican in front of them."

I knew exactly what Eva was talking about—people who try to make you ashamed. I was about to tell her about the same type of girls at my high school, then I remembered.

"One time I did this poetry reading at a Chicana writers' conference."

"Yeah?"

"And this woman asked me something in Spanish."

"And?"

"And when I answered her in my choppy Spanglish, she got really offended and uppity on me, totally made me feel like I didn't belong there."

"Was she Mexican?"

"Yeah, well, Chicana."

"They're the worst."

"Yeah, I mean, I felt so bad, Eva. I felt like shit. And the worst part was I heard her commend this white man on his sad little attempts with Spanish."

"You know"—Eva shoved the last of her sandwich into her mouth—"that's just another privilege for white people, they're allowed to fuck up and they still get the credit and encouragement, especially all these white politicians who start their speeches in shitty Spanish. The crowds always go so crazy! And how about Oprah? Like when she did that special on the Macarena or whenever she has Gloria Estefan or those two white women that cook Mexican food? Everyone thinks it's so great when she speaks shitty Spanish just because she's trying. That's so fucked."

I turned away from Eva. I couldn't believe that nearly two years later I was still feeling so lousy about the Chicana writers' conference. I quickly pulled my sunglasses over my eyes. I looked over at the White Socks, then over at Eva. She had pulled down her sunglasses, too.

By the end of the month I couldn't take the White Socks anymore. The program coordinator hadn't returned my calls and Señora Saldana refused to offer me the vacant room she had on the second floor.

"That's Bernardo's room," she explained. "He's coming next month from Italy and he always stays in that room."

"Can I rent it till he arrives?"

"Oh, no, Bernito wouldn't like that. No, no."

One day I came home to the sounds of Slutty Sock and a visiting boyfriend wailing along to Jane's Addiction. Their off-key cries filled the courtyard. Maybe if it hadn't been Jane's Addiction, I could've dealt with it. Maybe not. But it was definitely the final straw. That afternoon, I went on my own to look for a new place to rent and by the early evening I found a divorcée named Lara ready to rent out a single room with a bath. The minute we talked I instantly detected a catty competitive streak in her and liked it. She quizzed me about Señora Saldana's house—how clean it was, how Señora Saldana's diet was going, did she still have that sixty-inch Sony TV that her son-in-law got at the Wal-Mart in Mexico City? I knew she was jealous that Señora Saldana had a bigger house that allowed more students to rent from her, thus increasing her monthly income. I encouraged Lara's weakness and fed her exaggerated stories of an overcrowded house with weak water pressure and a refrigerator crammed with expired crema and petrified tortillas. I told her how I often found chicharrón crumbs on the kitchen counter every morning, evidence of Señora Saldana's midnight snacking. Lara just shook her head, clicking her tongue in pleasured disgust.

As a renter in Lara's home, I immediately felt like a part of her household, which consisted of her and a live-in helper (not *maid*), Tere. In mid-March, Lara invited me to a local wedding and she claimed anyone who was someone was going to be in attendance. So, of course, it infuriated her a week later when she discovered that Señora Saldana had also been invited.

But once the actual wedding day came, Lara and I spent the whole afternoon getting ready for the evening's event. She loaned me a black lace hankie to wear in the church and I lent her my Guess? sandals (okay, bought way before I heard anything about their labor "practices").

After the church ceremony everyone went to a local hotel for the reception. Both Lara and I saw Señora Saldana show up with three White Socks in tow. Lara had only one student—me. "But, hey"—I nudged her in the ribs with my elbow—"I'm *brown*."

A long-winded toast by an inebriated best man ("He's from the north," Lara explained later. "Todos alcohólicos.") was followed by a five-course dinner, the cutting of the cake, and dancing. I was amazed to witness so many brown boy guests showing off their regional expertise with loose hips and fast feet yet nary a bead of sweat drip from their foreheads. They desperately vied for attention from the White Socks and I immediately felt lonely and out of place while I watched the White Socks' sweaty bodies get fanned by the cloth napkins of the local boys. Finally Lara grabbed my hands and we created a group of single women who danced in a circle. It was actually pretty fun. It was just like the old days at the Odyssey 'cept none of the nearby dancing men were wearing eyeliner or lip-synching Duran Duran. Lara pointed out later that Señora Saldana had done the same thing but that her circle was much, much smaller.

Later, when we got home, I was in my room getting ready for bed, when I discovered Lara had stashed three small bottles of tequila in my purse as well as six recuerdos, little plastic bags filled with heart-shaped chocolates. Lara was still up watching TV when I found her secret stash. I entered the kitchen, waved my purse in front of her, and smiled. She smiled back, embarrassed. We stayed up, watching a rerun of *Marisol* and sucking the liquor out of the chocolate hearts. We then shared one bottle of tequila. And then a second one. She told me Señora Saldana's dress was tighter than the time she wore it to last year's big wedding and I laughed. Then I told her about one of the White Socks asking about the bowl-shaped tostadas, like at El Torito, but she just looked confused. As much as I tried to explain the humor in it, she didn't quite understand.

My Spanish was getting better, but not fast enough. Every homework assignment returned to me was marked up with red ink, looking like our instructor had just had a nosebleed all over it. I was told to talk with a local named G. Rod.

"G. Rod?" I asked. "What kind of name is that?"

"It's short for Geraldo Rodriguez," another student told me. "Talk to him. He's better than any ol' tutor."

I met G. Rod near the stand where the local Indians sold wooden bowls and silver bracelets. I learned I could score pot, stolen phone cards, and naked pictures of a brunette Daisy Fuentes from him.

"Next week I should have bootleg Christian," he bragged

But what I really wanted from G. Rod was a new textbook. Mine wasn't any help at all.

"You sure these are the right answers?" I questioned him suspiciously as I looked at each page in his book. Next to every exercise, the answers were written in pencil.

"Oh yeah," he assured me. "The old person that had this graduate with good grades and he live in Spain now."

The book turned out great. I found how easy it was to raise your hand in class when you knew the answers. I arrived to my sessions with great enthusiasm and clicked my tongue and shook my head slowly whenever the White Socks got answers wrong. Probrecitas blanquitas! I had the most free time of any of the other students and took Mati out to lunch twice a week.

I was on top of el mundo until I saw it. The name of the book's former owner. It was written on the last page of the book. How could I not have noticed it before? J. Randall. The old owner was named J. Randall. What kind of name is J. Randall? Masculine or feminine? It didn't matter. Randall was definitely not Mexican, not of color. It reeked of whiteness. Here this J. Randall knew all the right answers in Spanish and I didn't. What could be worse? I felt so ashamed, but I knew what I had to do. I walked to the nearby river that flowed near our school and I held the book high over my head. I flung the text into the roaring water.

Yeah, right. I'm not *that* dramatic. I actually sold the book to Miles, this British kid whose Spanish was slightly worse than mine. He paid triple the amount I had.

I may be Spanglish, but I'm not stupid.

It was my last week in Mexico and Lara wanted to treat me to dinner. "I want to take the bus into Iguala and treat you to pijones," she said.

Iguala was forty-five minutes south of Taxco. I had never been there and I had never heard of pijones. I mentioned this anticipated dining experience to an instructor and she remarked, "Pijones? How glamorous!"

I mentioned the dinner to the White Socks during a study break.

"Do you even know what pijones are?" Dandruff Sock asked, scratching the back of her scalp.

"Of course," I answered, and quickly changed the subject. "So where's Señora Saldana taking you guys for your good-bye dinner?"

"Nowhere yet," Clinique Sock answered. "We probably won't even be taken anywhere. I mean, there's twelve of us now and I don't think she could afford to take us all out."

"Oh, that's too bad," I responded.

Lara and I arrived in Iguala three o'clock on a Saturday. The restaurant was only about five blocks away from the bus station.

"Let's sit outside," she told me once we got there. "It's nice out."

It was nice out. But after a short while the late-afternoon sun was beating down on us. We looked for a table with an umbrella that wasn't covered in pigeon shit and after a few minutes, we gave up and sat inside, near an open door.

Lara was so animated. I could tell this was a big deal for her. Taking a bus ride out of town and treating me to dinner. She ordered us beers and sometime later, when she looked over my shoulder, I could tell from her expression that our food was coming to our table. I sat up and cleared my space for it.

A large white plate was set before me topped with a small green salad, a fan of avocado and lime slices, and there, smack in the middle, were the pijones. The glamorous pijones ricos were staring me straight in the eyes—or they would have, if their eyes were open, that is. But they weren't. They were closed, because these pijones, these pigeons, were dead! I looked down at two charred pigeons on my plate, which were inches away from my nose, and you better believe miles away from my fork. There was no way I was gonna eat pigeons.

Lara tore a wing off her own pijon and started chewing.

"What's wrong?" she asked. "Eat up, eat up!"

"Yeah, mmm, yummy," I answered. I took a corn tortilla from the basket and when Lara wasn't looking, I nonchalantly covered the birds with it. But when I looked down I was horrified to discover that the tortilla resembled a blanket and now the dead pijones looked like they were merely napping.

Since I didn't want to wake the pijones from their sweet dreams of one day flying to the top of the Statue of Liberty, I decided to pick at my salad. Slowly I nibbled on the lettuce and tomato rings, then I worked on the avocado slices. Anything so I wouldn't have to look down at my plate. Anything not to look at the napping pigeons. I took a sip of my beer and looked out onto the street. I saw a handful of their gray brothers fighting in the gutter over a single limp french fry.

Oh God, wasn't it time to go? Wasn't our bus leaving yet? On the other hand, I felt so guilty because I knew this was a big deal and a costly excursion for Lara.

"Come, come on," she urged me with her hand, the hand that didn't have a piece of pigeon in it. "Muy deliciouso, no?"

No. But of course I didn't say that. After a short while my salad was finished, the avocado slices had been consumed, and there were no more tortillas. There was nothing I could eat except the napping pijones that slumbered on my plate. I picked at the breast of one of them and I tried think of something, anything else, bowling scores, the cute boy at the wedding, should I give

Lara my Guess? sandals? I had to think of anything but eating the pijones.

"What's wrong?" Lara asked.

"Nothing," I answered, and put the piece of pijon down on my plate. "I'm just sorta full."

"Full? Already?" Then she looked suspicious. "You don't like them, do you?" she asked slowly.

"No, of course I do. We actually eat these back home, all the time. For Sunday dinner. I guess it's, well, making me sad to eat them again, 'cause, see, my grandma used to make these, like in a casserole, and she's dead now and . . . well, I've sorta been trying to cut down on my pijon intake and you know, they're high in cholesterol and . . ."

Lara reached over to my plate with a smirk on her face. She grabbed the head of one of my pijones and twisted it off. She stuck the whole thing in her mouth and rolled it around. When the waiter came to our table, she pushed the pijon head to one side of her mouth with her tongue and told him, "We'll take hers to go."

By late April, my program had ended and I decided to leave Taxco early on a Friday morning. The White Socks asked me to join them in Acapulco before heading home.

"We can go parasailing, and get our hair braided and there's even an IHOP on the main strip," PMS Sock informed me. "Come on, how long has it been since you've eaten at an IHOP?"

This week? I never had confessed to my secret visits to the IHOP in Cuernavaca, but I declined their invitation and told them I was anxious to get home. We all hugged and promised to be friends forever. Clinique Sock gave me her remaining Clarifying Lotion #2 and Slutty Sock shook her finger in front of my face: "You better not write about me in any of your stories!"

"I won't, promise."

The morning I finally left Taxco, Lara gave me a watercolor painting and her helper, Tere, gave me a silver ring. It was almost like a ceremony near the bus when Tere took the ring off her finger, said some words in Spanish, and slipped it onto one of mine. I felt my eyes start to water, but then felt foolish. I remembered seeing a mason jar full of cheap silver rings on Tere's nightstand. I imagined she handed every departing student one, it being the same ring she conveniently wore during their duration as a renter.

As soon I got comfy in my bus seat, I thought of returning home. I just knew Aunt Alma would have a barbecue in my honor and everyone would be there, in her backyard, hopping over all the fresh holes that Warlord had dug and checking the bottom of their shoes for dog shit that Warlord had, well, you know. Uncle Manny would stroll in with a case of Coronas on his shoulder and Tía Annie would say I'd gotten too dark and God forbid, everyone would think I really went away to work in the fields. Cousin Benny would comment, "Just 'cause you lived in Mexico don't be thinking you're all bad and that you know everything about Mexico and Mexicans and be correcting my already good Spanish."

As the bus crept out of the station, I nibbled on a salt cracker and waited for my Dramamine to take over. On the way out of Taxco I saw three minibuses coming in on the narrow main road. I was on Tres Estrellas, the huge premier bus line, and I wondered why we moved over to the side of the road to let the minibuses by. When I recognized them as being American study-abroad-program buses, I immediately knew why. I watched the minibuses, filled with students anxious for total immersion, enter Taxco. And just like four months earlier, the locals waved them in, with stars and dollar signs in their eyes. I watched from my seat, nibbling on a second cracker, as the annual blessing of mini blue buses, givers of life and opportunity, commenced on the main road into Taxco.

Role Model Rule Number 8

Reclaim Your Rights As a Citizen of Here, Here

I can't get by one week without a white person asking me The Question:

> *"So, where are you from?"*
> *"From Oxnard," I answer.*
> *"No, I mean originally."*
> *"Oh, St. John's Hospital, the old one over on F Street."*
> *"No, you know what I mean!"*

No, what do you mean? And why is it important to you and why do you really need to know? When Latinos ask me where I'm from, it really doesn't bother me. I can't help but feel some sort of familiar foundation is being sought and a sense of community kinship is forming. "Your family's from Cuernavaca? And what? They own the IHOP on Via San Robles? Wow, we really need to do lunch sometime!"

But when whites ask me The Question, it's just a reminder that I'm not like them, I don't look like them, which must mean I'm not from here. Here, in California, where I was born, where my parents were born, and where even my great-grandmothers were born. I can't help but feel that whites always gotta know the answer to everything. It's like they're uncomfortable not being able to categorize things they're unfamiliar with and so they need to label everything as quickly and neatly as possible. Sometimes when I'm asked The Question, I like to lie and make up areas within the Latin world from where I supposedly originated.

WHITE PERSON #1: So, where did you say you're from?

ME: From Enchiritova, it's actually a semi-populated islet off the coast of Bolivia.

WHITE PERSON #2: Yep! I knew it! I knew it! Kevin, didn't I tell you I thought she was an Enchirito!

WHITE PERSON #1: Tag her!

Now, instead of getting uncomfortable, I either immediately return The Question to the person who's asking, or I try to beat a willing white person to the punch.

ME: So where are *you* from?

EL OTHER: Me?

ME: Yeah.

EL OTHER: Oh, I'm from here.

ME: From Los Angeles?

EL OTHER: No, from here, *here*.

ME: You mean the corner of Venice and Inglewood?

EL OTHER: No, silly. You know what I mean.

ME: No, what do you mean, really? Where you from?

EL OTHER: Uh, I—I don't know.

ME: So what's your ethnicity?

LA OTHER: Oh, I don't got no ethnicity.

ME: Everyone has an ethnicity.

LA OTHER: No, I mean, I'm like a total mutt!

ME: A mutt? Come on, don't say that. That's like calling yourself a dog.

LA OTHER: Well, I am. I got so much of every kind of blood I couldn't even begin to tell you.

ME: You got any African?

LA OTHER: Of course not!

ME: So are you originally from the U.S.?

EL OTHER: Why?

ME: Just wondering.

EL OTHER: Well, my mother is French-Canadian and my father, his family's actually from Iowa. Wait, no, they're from Idaho.

ME: So what's your father's ethnicity?

EL OTHER: American.

ME: No, ethnicity. Not nationality.

EL OTHER: Uh . . .

ME: You don't know?

EL OTHER: Uh, no, not really.

ME: And where are you from?

LA OTHER: I'm from here actually. One of few people who can actually say they're native Californian.

ME: Your parents as well?

LA OTHER: Of course, . . . I'm sixth-generation Californian!

ME: Sixth-generation Californian? Wow, you don't look Mexican.

But one of the most insightful pieces of dialogue I had came from a conversation with a gentleman on an airplane. We were both flying to North Carolina. The in-flight movie was over, there were no magazines in the pouch in front of me and the batteries in my CD player were dead. Could striking up a conversation with my fellow passenger be so bad?

ME: So, where are you going? (Looking at his briefcase)
EL OTHER: To Raleigh, just on business.
ME: And where you from?
EL OTHER (looking out the window): From here.
ME: Oh . . . the Midwest?
EL OTHER: No, I'm from here. You know.
ME: What do you mean, *here?*
EL OTHER: I mean, I'm from here, here.
ME: Oh, I just meant originally. You look like . . . I don't know—different.
EL OTHER: What?
ME (fearing air rage): Oh, never mind.
EL OTHER: Different? Different as in how? That's the weirdest thing I've ever heard! No one has ever said I looked like I was from somewhere else! I'm American— American, from *here, here!*

He then turned his back to me and continued to look out the window. I suddenly felt awkward and I regretted subjecting him to my questionnaire. I meekly put on my headphones, closed my eyes and pretended to be listening to music. Before I knew it the pilot announced we should prepare for landing and as I put my seat back in its upright position, I looked over at the man. He was still looking out the window and I saw him exhale slowly. It was then I suddenly felt sorta sorry for him. It's amazing how many white people don't know anything about their own ancestry or background and so it's no wonder a lot of them confess to feeling so culturally bankrupt. A lot of white people get really defensive when you ask them where they're from. The Question is answered with an uncomfortable series of pauses, wrinkled brows and temple rubbing. They're confused when The Question is put upon them, because after all, they look like they're from good ol' "here," rather than some faraway "there." As our plane touched the ground I looked over at the man again and wondered how he knew where he was going if he didn't know where he was from?

I Know What You Did Last Summer

The following is based on the actual diary of a twenty-seven-year-old Chicana Lollapalooza Road Poet.

It is not a definitive statement on the middle-class, alternative-music scene. It does not offer any solutions.

It is, however, a highly personal chronicle and may provide insight into the complicated world we live in.

Names, dates, and places have been changed in accordance with the wishes of those concerned.

Dear Diary,

I can't believe I was picked! Two months from now I will be on the road, touring with Lollapalooza. Yay! Beth says they were supposed to have Nirvana, but since they couldn't make it (sad), they will now do the spoken-word thing. Unknown poets instead of Nirvana, I don't see the connection. Anyway, who cares. I get to go on the road! I get to read my poetry to stadium crowds across the country and guess what? I will get paid! Can you believe it? I will keep a record of the whole experience and then I will have documentation of all my exciting adventures. Oh, but what if someone finds you? Oh God, dear diary, that could be hell. Some people just don't have the respect for other people's privacy. I guess I could use code names. Like symbols or maybe write everyone's name backward. No, I'll use no names, just like in *Go Ask Alice.* Then, in case someone finds you, my dear sweet best friend, they won't know I'm writing about them and then shun me like Harriet the Spy. Beth, oops, I mean——says she thinks the Beastie Boys are gonna be on this tour. I hope so. That—— is so cute. This is gonna be the best summer of my life!

Dear Diary,
July 4——today was the first day of the tour. We were in Las Vegas and it was 117 degrees. Can you believe it? I saw two boys faint outside of the mist tents. Part of my job as a Road Poet is to read poetry all the time, anytime. The heat was so painfully uncomfortable . . . I changed three times cuz my clothes were just saturated with sweat. So, twelve of us will tour as Road Poets, but when we get to a new city, local poets will be added to that venue. One of the perks as a Road Poet is getting to eat for free at any of the food stands and——from Big Belly Burritos told me to come by anytime for free food. I asked him if there was lard in the burritos and he said no way and then when I said oh that's too bad, he laughed and said he'd throw in some lard just for me. He's pretty cute. If only he wasn't working a food stand.

Dear Diary, (Denver)
Every night——comes by the buses to deliver a stack of cheese pizzas and cases of beer. And sometimes——, who's hanging with the Beasties, comes by with a chunk of pot the size of a brick

and this is like eleven P.M. every night! I'm not even eating or smoking any of it. I want to stay in shape, I want to stay focused 'cause I have a lot of work ahead of me and I want to do a good job.

Dear Diary, (Kansas City)
Today was the greatest day. Hey, I sound like——from the Smashing Pumpkins! How can I not? I hear that song every single night before getting into this bunk to fall asleep into sweet nothingness. There are ten of us on this bus and it's really like a slumber party every night. We crank up the tunes, flash the hallway light off and on, and dance in the back end of the bus. All the other poets are so fun and nice. Today——helped me cut pieces of flannel for my "Grunge on a Stick." What I've done is taken Gene's old flannel shirts (one green, one brown) and cut them into one-inch squares. I skewer them on a bamboo stick and then roll a whole bunch of Teen Spirit (Baby Powder Soft scent) all over on them and then I sell them for twenty-five cents each. All these Midwest kids are buying them up! They always ask why some are green and some are brown and I just tell them, "Well, legally I can't say, but if I were you, I'd buy the green one. Ha, ha, ha! I got them believing they're ——'s old flannels when——gave them all away after his suicide. Anyway, today I sold a book! Can you believe it? This girl actually gave me six bucks for my book! I mean, she could have bought a hemp bag or a beaded choker or even a Big Belly Burrito, but no, she bought my book. This is going to be the best summer! See ya!

Dear Diary, (St. Paul)
What a horrible day. Today I read poems to only two people in the poetry corner and they weren't really in the corner to listen

to poetry, but were just waiting to use the Porta Potti. They always put the outhouses by the poetry corner, so there's all these people who aren't into poetry and who just gotta take a piss and sometimes they yell things. It's sorta demeaning to be reading in a place called "the corner." I mean, why can't it be called "the stage," or "the arena," or even "the space"? "Corner" sounds so infantile and unprofessional. Being in a corner reminds me of school when I was sent to stand once cuz I talked too much and I had to stand in it to learn how to be quiet. Ugh. Anyway, there were these guys, waiting to use the Porta Potti, and they were screaming at me to just shut up and show them my tits. I pretended not to hear them, but between you and me, dear diary, it was really hard not to. Today more poets had trash thrown at them on the main stage. Thank God it wasn't my turn to read.

Dear Diary, (Milwaukee)
I thought this was supposed to be like the granddaddy of alterna teen concerts, but everyone looks the same! I mean, the SAME oversized wallet chains, the same manic panic dyed hair, skinny dreads on skinny blond boys, baby Ts with cute little sayings from the seventies. God, this seventies revival thing is longer than the seventies themselves! And all these little white kids wearing oversized Dickies and Ben Davis . . . I can't help but think of all the kids I teach over in Southgate or El Monte and how they aren't allowed to wear that type of clothing 'cause it makes them look like gang members. More privileges for the white Ticketmaster class, I guess.

Dear Diary, (St. Louis)
Last week I remember thinking I was the happiest person in the whole world, in the whole universe, in all of God's creation. Could

that have only been last week or was it endless light-years ago? Today, when——and I were waiting for the rest of the bus entourage, we talked cop shop with some state troopers. When I told them I was from L.A., they said they'd never want to work in L.A. and that the LAPD has to put up with so much shit. When I asked them what they meant, they said (and I quote), "Well, out here everyone talks American, but in L.A. you got your Orientals and your Mexicans and you gotta talk to them and none of them speak English good, and that's stressful, and every day having all that stress and confusion, no wonder you just wanna beat the shit out of people."

Dear Diary, (Chicago)
Sorry I haven't written for a while. It's been raining. Each time a drop of rain hits me, I can swear it's a tear making up for the ones I want to cry. I don't understand it because last night I was so happy. I ate six wonderful, delicious, mouthwatering, delectable, heavenly slices of pizza but when I woke up this morning I felt horrible. Maybe it's not a good idea to eat so late at night. I had really horrible dreams and now I'm depressed. Today they told us they can't have any more poets on the main stage cuz too much trash is being thrown at them and it's damaging stage equipment. So now we are relegated to stay in the corner, the poetry corner. All the other poets are really bugging the shit out of me. The male poets do nothing but scream and scream and go on about their penises. Everyone is reading stuff about O.J., Kurt, sex, or drugs. Nobody knows what Oxnard is and my stuff isn't going over very well. I'm actually looking forward to going home. So far this summer hasn't turned out like what I thought it would be.

Dear Diary, (Columbus)

My suede mini, the patchwork one, doesn't fit anymore. Neither do my cutoffs. I shouldn't eat the pizzas anymore, but it's really the only thing I look forward to. Today,——from Big Belly Burritos asked if I wanted to make extra money making burritos. He said he'd pay me seven bucks under the table. So now I roll burritos three hours a day. I like hanging out with his crew. They're really the sincerest people, besides the Tibetan monks, that I've met so far on this stupid tour, and I'm really their best roller. I saw——from the Breeders bite into a burrito that I personally rolled and it didn't split open at all. Well, enough of this chitty-chat and writie-write. I better help——think of some fun things for the little alterna teens to do tomorrow.

Dear Diary, (Cincinnati)

Yesterday the producers came to my "Grunge on a Stick" booth and told me I better get rid of them cuz——has crashed the tour and is on a rampage, going after anyone who is making money off her dead husband. I told them that my "Grunge on a Stick" has nothing to do with him, but rather the whole Seattle scene. What I didn't realize was that these little things have become the "hottest item" to buy at Lollapalooza and that the press has dubbed them "Shish-Cobains." I had no idea.

Oh, also yesterday all the Road Poets had an interview with MTV. I HATE talking about poetry. I mean, come on, what can you possibly say? It's like talking about sex, I'd rather just do it than talk about it. Ha, ha! No, but I never know what to say, cuz you sound either arrogant or boring or just plain show-offy. So I really didn't say much and when our segment was aired, I wasn't even mentioned. I felt really left out. Just like in Mr.——'s English class.

Dear Diary, (?)*

Today I went skateboarding with———. I bought me my own skateboard and then I had it signed by all the bands. He said I should pray that one of them dies of an overdose or something and then my board will be worth so much money. So anyway, we were surrounded by acres and acres of cornfields and the sun was setting and it was so nice. Until he asked, shouldn't you be at the corner reading your poetry? And then I felt guilty. But the thought of going back to the poetry corner and reading to stoned frat boys with tribal tattoos was just too depressing.

Dear Diary, (?)

Sorry I haven't written for a while. I've been depressed. We've been to so many places I've lost track of time and places. I called ———today long distance and cried when I heard her voice. When I told her I was working making burritos, she said, "Michele, you shouldn't be rolling burritos. You're there to read your poetry." But when I told her I liked the burrito makers more than the poets, and that I liked making burritos more than reading poetry, she just said, "You're making us all look bad." Later I didn't know if she meant I make other poets look bad or other brown people (of whom I haven't seen any in a long time) look bad. Oh, and today this girl BEGGED me for my all-access badge. I've seen her at the last three venues working at one of the feminist tables and she said, "Please, please, please, I have to meet———from the Smashing Pumpkins!" But when I casually mentioned to her that he was married, she said, "I don't wanna meet his wife, I just wanna fuck HIM." Oh, like I should have known better.

There are no dates or locations for the following material. It was recorded on single sheets of paper, set lists, place mats, etc.

Dear Diary, (?)

I'm taking a break from the tour. I'm sick of the poets and the poetry corner and all the male poets that scream, scream, scream. I decided to go into Ann Arbor with everyone from Big Belly Burritos. In order to get the ride I had to help break down their stand and now I still reek of onions and bleach. We had to all sit in the back of a U-Haul truck with no windows or air and I was warned that——wakes up in his sleep and pisses on people. I didn't sleep at all, all night.

Dear Diary, (NYC)

Oh, the New York poets are the best! Man, they must write and practice a lot. They can think up poems quickly and lay down rhymes and just recite them quick. I wish I could do that. I am so jealous. It's raining and there's mud everywhere and I've lost my favorite platforms. I really just want to go home. Only one more day to go. I saw——backstage and I hear she hands out candy in exchange for borrowing equipment. Her toenail polish is chipped. Tacky.

Dear Diary,

Well, the tour is officially over for me. What a summer! I don't want to hear or read anything in stanzas for a while. If I see one more burrito, I will throw up and if I hear that screaming intro for "Sabotage" one more time, *I'll* scream! I am writing this from the train. I decided to take a train home rather than fly. It will take three days and——said I was crazy to take the train back to L.A., but I don't care. I wanna see the country. I wanna take my time and think about things for a while. Right now I'm eating an orange yeast roll I bought from the snack machine and it is so, so delicious. I can feel its warmth and am actually experiencing the orange zest. It's a thousand times better, a million, trillion times better than all that catered crap they served us on tour. I'm sitting across from an Amish family and they look so content and stress-free. No airs or gimmicks. I mean, what's it like to be so disciplined and humble and use craftsmanship for practical reasons? What's it like making art not just to show off and get attention? I wonder what it would be like to live on an Amish farm. Could *I* live on an Amish farm? I will definitely check into that for next summer. Yes, I'm gonna make next summer the best summer of my life. See ya!

Any Press Is Good Press

Being a role model sometimes takes you to faraway lands: Chicago, New York, San Josie. You have a presentation to present, poems to recite, a dissertation to . . . dissert? Sometimes you get the five-star treatment, a fancy-schmancy hotel where white help helps with your coat and calls you by your last name, which is mandatory even if they don't know how to pronounce it correctly.

I always like to make up fake elongated Spanish-sounding surnames not only to make their job more challenging but to add a little diversity to their life. I've created a name that includes my grandmother's middle name, my mother's maiden name, and the name of a character from at least one Garry Marshall sitcom.

"Excuse me, you dropped your scrunchie, Ms. Michele Maria Ruiz de la Verne de Fazio."

"Oh, thank you."

* * *

Just last month I was asked to speak at a very distinguished university. Okay, it was actually a night class held at some public high school, and I got a call early in the morning from a woman named Lori regarding my presentation. Lori told me I'd be staying at her house, in order to save money, and she hoped I didn't mind. I'm as nice and gracious to Lori as I can be so early in the day, but after hanging up with her, I get to wondering what her house is like. Does she have premium channels? Bagels or tortillas? Does this Lori have kids, a dog, or a husband who's gonna pounce on my bed and wake me up at six in the morning? But none of this matters as much as knowing if Lori is white. I must find out as soon as possible. As much as I may pride myself as seeing "no cuh-la lines!" it's crucial to my reputation to find out if Lori is white. Why? Because I have a speaking engagement, an obligation to be prepared, a responsibility to look presentable, which means I must have my clothes ironed. If Lori is white, she isn't gonna have an iron, 'cause as everyone knows, white people don't iron. It's as simple as that.

"*An* iron?" Wrinkled white people always pose the question. "Whaddya need an iron for? If something's wrinkled, you just throw it back in the dryer on the fluff cycle for a bit."

"That's it?" I ask, amazed.

"That, or turn the hot water on in the shower and the steam will get all the wrinkles out."

"Turn on the shower? When nobody's taking a shower?"

"Yeah, just shut the windows, close the door, and let the shower run for like twenty minutes. Everyone does it."

No, most *white* people do it. So now I know who to blame for that severe drought we had here in California during the late eighties.

To be honest—and this is an embarrassing confession for a self-proclaimed super-starched Chicana—but the unification of an iron and ironing board in my house while growing up was almost non-existent. I rarely saw my mother ironing. We had one iron that was caked with black goo and the seared remains of a pink polyester shell. We also had one rickety ironing board that made a screeching sound every time we pried it open, which of course sent Mama Kitty running for cover. So, from whom did I learn the meaning of making a well-pressed statement? Who conditioned me to recognize the value of double creases? One answer. Martha Reyes. Years ago, as a preteen, she taught me a lesson I never forgot.

Martha Reyes was my childhood best friend who lived up the block. As kids, we dressed alike, talked alike, dug the same boys, and lied to all the same hall monitors. We had everything in common until that day we entered junior high and then the changes between us became apparent. Painfully apparent. Martha started to iron, *everything*—her Pendletons, the white T-shirts she wore under her Pendletons, the corduroys she wore with the white T-shirts, she even steamed the sides of the black winos that she started to wear religiously every day in place of her sneakers.

As a seventh grader, while I learned to grab things out of the dryer and throw them on while running out the door, Martha started choosing ironing-board covers that complemented her bedroom wallpaper.

When I mentioned Martha's ironing obsession to Patty Romero, she said, "Well, that's 'cause Martha's a chola now and they iron everything."

Later I asked Martha, "Are you a chola now?"

"Who said that?" she demanded. She was in her bedroom, hunched over the ironing board as usual and creating creases on the backs of her Levi's.

"No one."

"Someone from some other *clicka*—I mean, neighborhood?"

"Actually, it was Patty."

"Oh, well, what do you think?" she asked.

"Well, you sure do iron a lot."

"I just wanna look nice." The steam from the iron made her white powdered face turn pink.

"But why do you have to iron everything?"

"Because I want everything to look nice." She put the iron on its stand. "I wanna show you something."

I followed her to the hall closet and when she opened it, I couldn't believe what I saw. There, on the two shelves, among sleeve extensions, various cans of starch, and extension cords, were irons, so many irons they were lined up in two rows according to size. "You can't use the same iron for different clothes," she explained. She pulled one iron off the shelf. "This one, well, I just can't get rid of it. It still has some heat left to it and it's old, but you remember my aunt Ruthie? She loved this iron. She put pleats in everything and this iron always came through for her. She always looked so nice in her clothes. Too bad she was never actually able to see how nice she looked."

"What do you mean?"

"She was blind."

"She was blind? How could she iron?"

"Look." She put her hands over some bumps. "The settings are in Braille."

Martha pulled down another iron. "This one's left over from my sister's wedding. She got fifteen irons at her bridal shower. Can you believe that? Only fifteen! Anyway she kept eleven out of respect and gave the rest to family. I got this one. Look, it's still in the box, from May Company. Fancy, huh?"

"Yeah."

Next Martha showed me a heavy-looking chrome-and-black

contraption. "Now, this one is one bad ol' thing. It was my great-grandmother's. My mother's grandma." She pointed out the sharp tip that made a perfect V. "Check out the point on this thing."

"Yeah, it's sharp."

"They don't make 'em like this anymore. I use this one strictly for collars and cuffs and it heats up in less than ten seconds. In my great-grandma's will, she even requested that the dress she's buried in be pressed with this iron." Martha put the iron back on the shelf. "Oh, and look, check these out."

She rolled her sleeves up. "Shit, now I'm gonna have to re-iron the sleeves again. Anyway, check it out."

She showed me her wrists, which were covered with several raised dark burns. I had never noticed them before.

"Eew!" I looked away.

"It's nothing to get grossed out over," she snapped. "My mother has these scars, my grandmother had these scars. I can't even imagine being a Reyes without these iron bites. They're a permanent mark of excellence."

I looked at her burns. "Martha," I started to tell her, "I don't understand. Really, what's the big deal about having everything so perfectly ironed?"

"You really still don't get it?"

"Not really."

"Okay, I'll show you what the big deal is."

"Yeah, I wanna know."

We went back to her bedroom and she pulled out a shoe box from under her bed. In it was an assortment of snapshots, some dried flowers, and her sister's faded high-school graduation tassel. Martha dug through the box and pulled out one color photo. She held it to her chest. "Okay, you really want to know?" she asked again.

"Yeah, Martha, come on, what's the big secret?"

"Okay, remember when Anthony Rivera came to speak at our school? After Cinco de Mayo?"

"Of course I remember. It was the most exciting day of my life."

"Now, what I'm gonna show you may make you sick, it may shock you, but I'm only showing you to teach you a lesson."

"Okay, okay." I pretended to brace myself.

The picture Martha showed me was of herself. To one side of her was Mr. Evans, our principal, and to her other side was Anthony Rivera. Anthony Rivera, dancing sensation and former *General Hospital* star.

"Look at his suit, look close," she said.

Anthony was wearing a dark blue suit. Creases ran across his chest, and some gathered around each thigh. There were sweat rings under each arm.

"Perspiration pads would have taken care of that," she pointed out. "And extra starch near his knees would have prevented the creases. He should've thought ahead and known he was gonna be sitting in the car, waiting in a chair, before getting up to speak."

"God, he looks horrible!"

"Yeah, really ruins your impression of him, huh?"

"But on *GH* he looked so good."

"Yeah, well, they got people who take care of things like that, like with portable steamers."

"Portable steamers?"

"Oh, yeah, my mom ordered me one. It should be here next week, you should come check it out."

I looked at the photo again. "God, look at the wrinkles near the elbows, and his lapel, it has lines on it."

"Yeah, and you know the worst part of it is?"

"There's more?"

"This picture is gonna be around forever. I mean, after we're dead and after he's dead, someone's gonna find this picture and see how lousy he looked. Can you believe he went out looking like this and he's Mexican."

"Actually, I think he's Puerto Rican."

"Puerto Rican? Who told you that?"

"Margaret Simon."

"Really?" She looked at the photo again. "Well, anyway, what do you think of our Hispanic role model now?"

"If only he took the extra time to iron," I said. I suddenly saw Martha's point.

And it was because of that day, and those wise words from Martha's mouth, that I lay in my bed thinking about my presentation, thinking about Lori. Was she white? Would she have an iron? I picked up the phone and star-69'd her to find out.

Counter Act

"You're over an hour late!"

"An hour?" I put my back pack in my locker. "Dan, I'm scheduled for two o'clock."

"No, you were supposed to be here at one. Not five after two. You got customers waiting and Janson called. His order's all wrong and he's PISSED. Why didn't you call?"

Dan's always on my case. On my back, checking the little hand on the time clock, re-counting the minutes on my time card. Only two weeks out of the year do I breathe easy, feel my spine go straight, and experience an all-over calmness. Two weeks when Dan goes on his vacation, back home to Illinois.

"I didn't call 'cause I didn't think I needed to," I tell him. "Dan, I am scheduled for two. If I should've called for being five minutes *tar-dee* after my scheduled time, then I'm sorry. I couldn't find parking." I could never tell Dan the truth, that I had a mid-morning poetry reading way out in Bell Gardens, miles and at-

titude away from Santa Monica. I could never explain that I
decided, last minute, to indulge in the Tuesday lunch special of
pot pie and snickerdoodles, with a roundtable of junior-high-
school teachers discussing which books define the Latino experience, commuter mug holders that work best in cars with worn
shocks, and how to keep chalk prints off your ass.

"Where do you have this idea you were scheduled for two?"

"Dan, it's not an idea, it's a fact." I pull my wrinkled smock
out from the locker and try to flatten it with my hands.* "I told
Laura I was coming in at two. I told her three weeks ago in
writing. I had to get my cyst removed."

"Your what?"

"My cyst." I pull my smock over my head and pull my hair
out from under it. I scrunch my face to make myself look in pain.
"At first I thought I had hurt myself from work, with all the
heavy lifting and everything. But it turned out to be a cyst. The
doctor found it right on my ovaries, the size of a golf ball and—"

"Ugh." Dan grimaces. "I don't need the details."

"I thought you wanted to know what happened to me. Like I
told Laura, I needed to have my cyst removed or else I coulda had
some major complications. Ask Laura, she knows about the whole
schedule change."

"Laura's on vacation."

"Oh, she is? Oh, yeah, that's right." Of course I knew that.
Vacationing supervisors always give good excuse. They're never

---

*Sometimes role models have to take day jobs. Whether you're a counter girl
sporting a smock or an honored guest speaker in a power suit, you should always
try to look your best. It's all about "representin'!" (See Role Model Rule Number
9.)

around to confirm schedule changes and by the time they get back from wherever they were, they're in such a revitalized mood, with their little tans and their little snow domes that they place right on their desk, to show everyone where they've been. Returning supervisors will agree to anything. "Well, I don't know what to say," I continue with Dan. " 'Cept I'm sorry for being, what, five minutes late? I just better get down there and help Artie."

"Can you work? What about your cyst?"

"Dan, weren't you listening to what I just said? I don't have it anymore. I guess I could've rested at home but I didn't want to let Artie down. He goes crazy when he has to wait on customers. I better get down there."

When I get to my department no one is even around. Not one customer like Dan claimed to have seen waiting. Artie is in the back cutting a small yellow mat at the mat cutter.

"What happened to you?" He puts the mat down, takes off his glasses, and starts cleaning them. "I need to eat."

"Nothing happened to me, Artie. This is the time I was supposed to come in." I don't look directly at him but instead into my reflection in the mirror above the department's phone. Funny, how I can easily lie to myself, but not so comfortably to others, especially when I have to look into their eyes

"The schedule says one o'clock." He doesn't let up. "I haven't been to lunch and I've been waiting for over an hour for you to relieve me."

"So go." I look at him from the mirror. "What are you waiting for? I'll watch the counter."

I check my hair out and start fixing my barrettes. Bangs or no bangs? God, it drives me crazy.

"Did you hear me?"

"No, what?" I didn't even know Artie's still talking to me.

"I said, I'll be back in a half hour." He takes off his smock and makes his way past me.

Of course he won't be back in half an hour. He'll be back in twenty-nine and a half minutes. Old people are either on time or way early and even though Artie can never finish the big-ass seven-course lunches his wife makes him, he'll be back exactly when he says he will. Old people *never* lie.

As soon as he bails I go to the front counter and grab the service bell. We've had the service bell for only four months. Dan brought it to our department the day after Thanksgiving. He was so convinced we'd be more efficient with it. He said if we didn't wanna hear the bell, all we had to do was stay on our toes. "The bell shouldn't go off more than once by the same customer," Dan insisted. The bell was an asset to our department. The bell would regulate fine service. The bell is our best friend. Fuck the bell! I toss our best friend into a small box filled with Styrofoam shipping peanuts and begin to call Angela at home.

I'm thrown off by her voice on the machine. *Hey, you've reached Angie and Michele. We're not home right now. If this is Hardy, hey, I need directions for tonight. I won't be home till almost nine, so I'll be able to make it downtown by ten. If you want, come on by and meet me here. I'll leave a key under the duck, the little duck, not the big one. Okay? Or you can call me at work. Or if you want, you can . . . BEEP*

What's this about? She changed my outgoing message? I check the counter again and see only one woman looking at the mat samples. Cool. I dial Angela's work number.

After punching in all the extension codes I finally get Angela.

"Small purchases, this is Angie, may I help you?"

"Angela, it's me. What's up with the new outgoing message? Why did you take mine off?"

"Oh, I had to leave Hardy a message."

"Yeah, and everyone else who calls. Angela, you don't leave

messages on the machine telling people where you put the house key."

"Well, if they're calling, they gotta be friends. And if they're strangers, then they don't know where we live."

"Can you help me?" I look up and see the same woman at the counter. I nod at her, turn my back away from the counter, and keep talking to Angela.

"So where you going tonight?"

"Oh, just this party. Bobby G. is in from school and Linda Moore is gonna have a little thing for him. No big deal."

"Oh, I know Bobby. He's funny." *Invite me, ask me to go.*

"Yeah." She yawns. "He sure is. I can't wait to see him."

"So, hey, I had this great reading today."

"Really, where was it at?"

"Sorta by South Central." *Sounds street, that'll impress her.*

"South Central?" she asks suspiciously. "*Where* in South Central?"

"Just this space. It was sorta an academic crowd." She didn't need to know exact details.

"Did they pay you?"

"Well, they took me to lunch . . ." *Just with teachers, but still they asked me to join them.*

Suddenly I hear Dan's voice. "Let me get someone for you, ma'am. Michele, will you come help this customer?"

I hang up quickly with Angela and go to the counter. I see the same woman there. "Oh, I'm sorry," I tell her. "I thought you were still deciding on colors."

She throws me a look like she knows what I'm about and then Dan throws me a look like he's gonna deal with me later.

"I bought this in Egypt," the woman explains as she flattens out a papyrus piece on the counter. It's an imprint of two skinny pharaohs and some even skinnier-looking dogs at their feet. "It's very fragile," she tells me. "Have you ever worked with papyrus before?"

"Oh, yes." I clear away the mat samples left behind from the last customer. What did she think? I mean, they sell this papyrus shit all over Venice Beach, stacks of them they can't get rid of, and what does she mean, "I bought this in Egypt"? Okay, lady, so you've traveled.

"I want a thick black lacquer frame for it. Everything in my house is white with black lacquer." She squints her eyes and holds the papyrus piece with a corner frame sample up and away from her.

Solie, the other girl who works mornings, told me when I first started working at Alexander's that blacks always want black lacquer frames. "Then you got your whites," Solie explained. "They like beechwood, all that whitewashed shit." She pointed to the samples on the wall as if she was a tour guide or something. "They always want that Southwest look for their Palm Springs pad. But the Mexicans . . ." And she placed her hand on her chest as if she was bragging or something. "Well, we like gold."

I took the last preference as a note of achievement. Everyone knows that gold is the best. Gold wood frames are the most expensive, the most difficult to join at the corners, and only Mexicans are savvy enough to recognize this value. "Look at this one." Solie held up a corner sample of an ornate gold-leafed wood molding. It looked like a knickknack straight from the Vatican gift shop or the master bathroom at Tía Annie's house. "I got this frame for my mom," she said. "And, check it out; for a twenty-four-by-thirty-six, I got it *half off*. I framed a picture of la Virgen in it. Are you into la Virgen?"

"Uh, yeah," I answered, "of course." How do you answer a question like that? I mean, if you're "into" a saint? She smiled and her gold tooth showed. We've been pals ever since.

And now, after three years at Alexander's, I'm beginning to think that Solie is right. Or is it just a coinky-dink that here's another black person wanting a black lacquer frame for their home?

"What do you think of this one?" The woman shows me a thinner version of the same frame.

"Yeah, that one's nice." Come on, lady, I'm not working on commission. Who cares what I think?

"Well, let me see what my sister thinks." She looks around. "Oh, do you have a bathroom?"

"Yeah, you need to get the key from the back register."

When she leaves the counter I go back to the phone and start to redial Angela's number.

"What do you think you're doing?"

I don't even have to look up. It's Dan, again.

"I'm calling up orders," I tell him.

He looks around the counter. "Where's the bell that's supposed to be out here?"

"It should be out here." I hang up the receiver. "I could swear I saw it earlier."

"That lady had been waiting over ten minutes for you to help her."

"But, Dan, I was calling up orders."

"Even if you're on the phone calling up orders, as soon as you hear the bell, you're to get off the phone *promptly* and service the customer who's at the counter. You do not keep them waiting!"

"Dan, I know, I thought she was still looking at samples. I greeted her when she first came to the counter."

"No, you didn't. I saw your back toward her the whole time. Michele, don't argue with me. I was at register four watching the whole thing. That bell needs to be on the counter at all times."

I start to shift things around on the counter, helping him look for the bell.

"Maybe Artie accidentally moved it," I say. "Lemme check in the back."

I pretend to look for it on the back table when Dan calls out to me again.

"Michele, you have a customer waiting."

Man, I am not *even* in the mood for this!

I walk out and it's Nikki Chase standing there on the other side of the counter. Shit, I'd much rather deal with the woman and her papyrus straight outta Egypt.

"Hey, what a surprise!" Nikki actually looks more shocked than surprised. "I didn't know you worked here!"

"Oh, hi, Nikki." I try to sound casual. "I didn't know you lived out this way."

"I don't," she answers. "I hate the Westside. I go to Loyola and I'm just between classes. My next class starts in a couple of hours. What about you? Where'd you end up transferring to?"

"I haven't transferred yet, really."

"Michele, are you serious?" She raises her eyebrows. "God, you were at SMC before *I* got there. Don't tell me you're becoming a professional JC student!" She puts her hand over her mouth to cover her laugh.

"No, no. Nothing like that." I try to smile. "I'm transferring in the fall."

"You're always transferring 'in the fall.' Come on, how long have you been saying that?"

"No, really I am. I'm going to school in New York." *Yes! Good one.*

Her tone becomes a little bit more serious. "Oh really? Where to?"

"Columbia," I answer. Just like that. My eye doesn't twitch, no skip in my voice. Nothing. Damn, I didn't think I lied good to people.

"Columbia! You're . . . going to Columbia? I don't believe it. I mean, what are you studying?" She looks so astonished, so . . . so humbled. *Double yes.*

"Yeah, well I'm gonna be studying creative writing."

All that time I spent with Nikki in the math lab at SMC all she could talk about was Columbia. "I'll just die if I don't get into Columbia," she used to say. "I mean, I just *have* to live, study, and breathe Manhattan. I mean, West Coast colleges can't even compare to what's going on with the East Coast. I mean, they are so ahead." Then I'd answer her with a fake yawn, "Yeah, about three hours ahead, right, Nikki?"

"Oh, that's right, you want to be a writer," she continues. "But I mean, wow, you never mentioned anything about wanting to go to Columbia when we used to study together. That's really great, Michele. Wow, I'm really happy for you."

Any more "wows"? And so what if I never mentioned it? People change their mind all the time. People make new plans. Please, Nikki, just leave. I don't want to talk with you anymore.

"So, funny we run into each other, huh? I had no idea you worked here."

"Just part-time," I tell her. "I mean, whenever they need extra help. I'm sorta on call."

"Oh, how funny." Her eyes scan the wall of frame samples. "Ooh, that one's nice. How much would a frame cost for something like that in an eight-by-ten?"

"Which one?"

"That one, third from the left and the fourth down." She gets on her tippy toes to point out her selection across the counter.

"Oh, the whitewashed oak one?" I smile to myself and pull the sample from the wall.

"Oooh." She takes it and looks at it closer. "My mother would *love* this."

"Does she have wood like this in her house?" I ask.

"Not really," Nikki answers. "But our condo in Palm Desert is filled with white, bleached wood like this."

Check out my girl Solie! She really does know her shit!

"Well." I look up the frame in the price book. "For an eight-by-ten, it'll run you about thirty-two bucks."

"Thirty-two bucks?" she answers. "You gotta be kidding! And then there's the labor charge, right?"

"Exactly." I gloat. "That's another eight bucks." Don't even try to work a deal.

"Hmmm, I just don't know. I just came in looking for a little something for my mom. Then I thought a frame or something would be cute, but now I just don't know. What are you getting your mom?"

"My mom?"

"Yeah, for Mother's Day."

"Oh, yeah, that's right."

"Don't tell me you forgot about Mother's Day? Oh, God, Michele, nice daughter you are!"

And that's when it happens. I immediately feel cold and numb. The lower part of my stomach slowly begins to hurt and my mouth feels suddenly dry. And all this petty superficial counter chitchat Nikki and I just exchanged becomes meaningless, nothing. Ol' Nikki Chase and her successful university transfer. Ol' Nikki Chase and her aspiring academic career at Loyola Marymount means jack 'cause right now, this minute, I'm reminded of what she has and what I haven't. Nikki Chase has a mother and I do not.

"Well, don't let me keep you from your work," she interrupts my sudden sadness. "You go back to what you were doing and

I'm just gonna look around the store for something else. This frame just ain't gonna do it, money-wise. But I'll come back to say bye before I leave."

Just then Artie returns back from lunch.

"How was the counter?" he asks me.

"Fine. No sales." I'm not paying attention and my stomach begins to hurt more.

"I have some leftover chicken from lunch," Artie tells me as he starts to put on his smock. "You're welcome to have it later for your dinner break. It was my son's birthday yesterday, so there's even some cake. You want it later tonight?"

If I know Artie's wife, it'll all be in little Tupperware containers. And everything will be separated by food groups in their little plastic compartments and it will remind me of my mother, how she was a Tupperware lady and would sometimes put together my lunches for school and how I'd be so embarrassed 'cause I just wanted a regular-type lunch in a regular brown bag. But nothing my mother did was regular, including my birthday cakes. Last year, even though her health had taken a turn for the worse, she baked my cake from scratch. It was practically eleven inches high with super-sweet pink-and-orange frosting and while it was carried out to the kitchen table, she had to stay reclined on the living-room couch. She was just too sick. I know she would have clapped along as I blew out the candles and wished my wish, if she could, but her hands, they were just too weak.

Please, God, I remember wishing, *don't let this be the last birthday, don't let this be the final cake from her. Please just make her better, healthy again, and I promise, come October I will bake her a birthday cake twice as high.*

But I guess I must've shared my wish with someone 'cause it didn't come true. She never did get better and died three months, four days later.

Now the thought of eating Artie's son's birthday cake made by his own mother is too unbearable. The side of my stomach begins to hurt more. While I put back the frame samples that Nikki had just looked at, I answer him. "Oh, no thank you, Artie, I really don't feel that great."

"Is it your cyst?" he asks.

"My what?"

"Is that the right word?" he asks as he rubs his hands back and forth nervously. "Dan mentioned that you had an operation, in your . . . stomach. Are you in pain?"

"Yeah," I tell Artie. "Sometimes I'm in a lot of pain and I don't realize just how much pain until it hits me much, much later."

Twelfth Call

"Mr. Chavez!"

"Yes?"

"Oh, I'm so happy to have reached you! You're a hard man to pin down!"

"Who is this?"

"Oh, sorry. This is Michele, Michele Serros."

"Who?"

"Michele Serros, you had me read at your luncheon back in May."

"Oh, yes. Now is not a good time for me to talk. What can I do for you?"

"Well, I haven't received my check, for my reading."

"Oh, no. I wish I would have known earlier, because now our funds are nearly depleted."

"But I've been calling you."

"I haven't gotten any of your messages."

"Well, uh, I still need my payment. I mean, the agreement was I would be paid after my reading."

"Yes, but if we don't have the money, we don't have the money. There's nothing I can do."

"But you had the money back then, I don't understand."

"Look, I'm in the middle of organizing the Hispanic Literature Series. Let me call you after the weekend and I'm sure we can straighten this whole thing out then."

"But—"

"Mira mi'ja, let me just call you next week and I promise to get your money to you. But you know, *I* don't do any of this for the money."

Distinguish the Difference Between a Great Contact and a Good Connection

I received the invite in early September. It was on heavy cream-colored paper with ragged edges like some fancy wedding invitation. It didn't have a postage stamp of two white doves forming a heart and it didn't have that pastel-colored confetti tucked inside that spilled on my carpet upon opening. No, the flair went as far as the ragged edges. And this invite, bold and businesslike, was from a women's television network, America's Number One Women's Television Network, the return envelope claimed. The network was requesting my presence at a national focus group for women and wouldn't I want to participate in their three-day conference? Wouldn't I like an all-expenses-paid extended weekend in D.C.? How about hanging with over one hundred female luminaries in some posh hotel? So, since they considered me "a woman who makes a contribution to her community," and I needed a snow globe from D.C., I naturally checked the "yes" box on the reply card and mailed it back.

Angela said it all sounded so bourgie and boring. "You're gonna be stuck with all these women who married into privilege."

"Yeah, you're probably right."

"Pretending to have stuff in common with them, stuffing your face with crab cakes and champagne."

"That's for sure."

"Hey, can you get me an invite to this thing, too?"

I couldn't get Angela an invitation to the conference, but she was actually excited that I was asked to be a part of it. "Make sure you get lots of business cards," she said. "And definitely make lots of good contacts." Three months later I was in D.C. in a cute little brown maxiskirt I found at Ross. I kept the tags tucked in just in case I didn't spill any crab cake on my lap. I may have wanted to take the skirt back later, after the conference.

My first good contact was a girl I met at the first evening mixer. Her name was J.T. and she worked for Rock the Vote. I actually remembered her from the airport in Los Angeles. She was the one who set off the metal detector with her nose, tongue, and nipple piercings. We clicked instantly—she also was in her twenties and had the tag of her Marshall's blouse tucked in. Together we pooh-poohed the women in gold-buttoned power suits and helped ourselves to the first glasses of free wine that came our way. After just one glass each we both became relaxed and started mingling among a roomful of East Coast CEOs, highly decorated generals, and one bona fide former Miss America. (No, not the one found in nudie shots.) We all wore name tags, mine reading, "Chicana Poet, Los Angeles," which, thank God, eliminated anyone asking The Question (see Role Model Rule Number 8).

All of the attendees, of course, were women. Bold, vocal, opinionated women who were not shy about grabbing the complimentary pencils from behind their ears and scribbling comments on their clipboards. And for the next three days, that's what we did, talked and took notes in formal discussions—contemplating glass ceilings, the future of breast feeding in the unemployment line, and what women's television programming really should be, between the douche and weight-loss commercials.

After three days of such intense focus we were all going to be honored by one grand finale dinner, one that would be filmed and later shown in snippets on America's Number One Women's Television Network. I checked my Ross skirt for any noticeable lap spills and J.T. applied her eyeliner heavier. "Just in case the camera points our way," she said.

But when J.T. and I entered the banquet hall that evening, we discovered there wasn't just one camera, but dozens of them, heavy-looking industrial-sized equipment with men in headsets behind each one. Almost every camera was directed toward one table that was strategically placed in front of the stage. It was clearly the table reserved for the bigwigs of the conference.

"I betcha that's the table that's gonna be on TV," J.T. pointed out.

We walked by the reserved table and started to make our way through the banquet room. It was filled with hundreds of circular tables, each topped with maroon-colored linen cloths and oversized floral arrangements. I thought of all the weddings I attended where you were allowed to take home the centerpieces. Does a four-foot-high winter foliage display count as carry-on?

Suddenly I felt a tap on my shoulder and I turned around. "Michele!" It was Julie, one of the coordinators from America's Number One Women's Television Network. "We have you sitting at the reserved table this evening."

"The reserved table? Me?"

"Yes, over here." She took my hand and started to lead me

toward the reserved table, but not until J.T. could quickly whisper in my ear, "You know why they asked you to sit there, don't you? They gotta have their little rainbow roundtable ready for their close-up on national TV."

I took J.T.'s comment as pure jealousy and followed Julie to the most important table of the room. I was immediately introduced to my dinner companions, a blind Native American college professor on my right and an Armenian physicist in a wheelchair to my left. I thought about J.T.'s comment. Hmmm. Gradually, however, more and more women in similar monochromatic double-breasted suits filled up the rainbow round table. I met a playwright who I'd seen featured numerous times in *People* magazine, an orchestra leader (with bad breath), and a Washington heavyweight with a bone-crushing handshake. I was surrounded by detailed chitchat about ski weekends in Aspen with Martha (Stewart) and how an old pal, George (Lucas), was so happy with a "prequel" he was shooting. I suddenly felt self-conscious. Oh, what could I possibly talk about with these women? What could I possibly say that would add value to their six-figure lives? "Hey, you know they got Kate Spade bags over at Ross for six bucks?" "Is that a real cell phone? But it's so small!" Yeah, right. So, after a horribly long thirty minutes of silence on my part, I thought I'd do what I always do when I'm in situations like that. I sought out those who I have something really in common with.

"Oh, are these shrimp-and-mango mini-quesadillas?" I joked with the waiter. "Just like our grandmas used to make, huh?"

"You're from Zacatecas?" I asked the bartender. "*My* family's from Zacatecas!"

"You really like it?" I questioned the second server. "I got it at Ross!"

*　*　*

After some time had passed, I could feel an overall sense of nervousness in the air and it wasn't just me anymore. We were all growing tense waiting for our mystery guest speaker, who hadn't shown up yet. It couldn't be Anthony Rivera, could it? Finally a woman with a slim stack of papers rushed over to our table. She was a skewer stick of a female, with short feathered, frosted hair, large eyes, and a very sharp pointed nose. She put her papers down on the table across from me, shook hands with the *People* playwright, and hugged the orchestra leader with bad breath. They were obviously friends, or at least colleagues. As she seated herself, she looked over my way, and I smiled. She smiled back and then told the server, "Just coffee," as she pushed aside her plate of wilted spinach salad and looked over her papers. She was obviously our honored guest speaker.

And then the woman kept looking around. That nervous kind of observation, like when you're at a party and you don't know anyone, so you keep looking for a familiar face to come rescue you from solitary. Or, like when you're at a party and you're already talking to a person you know and you're pretty comfortable with that person, but you're actually pretty bored so you keep looking over that boring person's shoulder, hoping you'll spot someone cooler to talk with. But I knew this woman wasn't just looking for cooler people to talk with—she was networking, looking for contacts. God, she was as desperate as me.

She looked over at my name tag and said, "Oh, you're a poet! And from Los Angeles! We *must* talk later." I told her "sure" and thought to myself, *Yeah, right, just as long as you don't take time away from me meeting more important people.* And then, that's when the rubbing started. She started to rub her nose. First a few swipes at the tip, then she brushed under it, left to right, right to left, quickly so no one would notice. She took another dainty sip from her coffee cup.

At first I thought that maybe she thought she had something hanging from the inside of her nose, and I really did feel for her. I know what it's like being in public with a feeling that something's clinging from the inside and that you really can't do anything about it. She kept playing with the tip of her nose and then I suddenly realized why she was really doing all that swiping. Not for fear of a booger, not for concern of dried postnasal drip, but for fear of residue—*blow* residue. You know, coke, cocaine, the evil white powder. Of course! That's why she was so nervous and that's why she was so skinny and *that's* why she was so late. She was in the bathroom doing lines. Oh, God—I looked around—could anyone else detect her secret?

I immediately thought that I shouldn't be at the same table with her. What if someone snaps a picture of us? What if the TV camera picks her up as my dinner companion? She could be bad for my aspiring role-model reputation. I immediately thought of my father, who always said you may not have money, you may not have fame, but you'll always have your credibility, and here this woman was jeopardizing my long running drug-free, just say no credibility. She might discredit a future of PSAs, a Gap ad, or my opportunity to make the back page of *Latina* magazine just because of *her* little socioeconomic problem. The Chicana Poet in Ross and the Coke Head in Chanel. Oh dear, I definitely had to sit at another table. But before I knew it, a bright white spotlight lit up our rainbow roundtable. Oh, God, I was gonna be seen on national TV with this woman! She smiled directly into the cameras and made her way up to the stage and waited for a second introduction to the podium.

As the applause echoed in the banquet hall, I realized that once the woman was done with her speech the camera would surely follow her back to the table. I looked around and saw J.T.'s table was filled up and that in fact every seat in the hall was taken. I began to feel more and more uncomfortable. There was no other place to sit. I finally pushed myself away from the table and decided just to leave the dinner altogether.

I felt another tap on my shoulder as I was exiting the banquet hall. I expected it to be Julie, but it wasn't. It was J.T. "Check you out," she whispered. "Sittin' with Cokey."

Cokey? Oh my God. Our guest speaker was nicknamed Cokey? J.T. was obviously more in the know than I thought.

"She's more into journalism than poetry," she continued. "But I think she'd be a great connection for you."

Connection?! What, did J.T. think I needed a coke connection from someone named Cokey? Do I have that *look*? Did she think all ethnic minorities were always searching for better *connections*?

"Look J.T., I don't need that type of connection," I snapped. "We have our own in *the barrio*!"

"What?" she asked, confused.

I held the side of my stomach. "Hey, my stomach hurts. I think it's my cyst. I think it's acting up."

"Oh shit, can I help you?"

I shook my head and just got away from her as fast as I could.

The next morning was frantic with noontime checkouts and shuttle-bus schedules, and I didn't get a chance to ask J.T. about the situation the night before. During the whole five-hour flight home, I thought about the conference and all the topics discussed and especially about J.T. and the guest speaker. How quick J.T. was to judge me and how quick I was to judge the guest speaker. I guess it didn't matter what class or race one may be, we all have our faults and problems. That woman had her own issues to deal with. Was I more critical because she was the honored guest speaker at a seemingly prestigious conference? Was I more surprised because she was wearing high-end clothing and appeared well-groomed and well-spoken?

And I almost forgot about that woman, the guest speaker who brushed her nose nervously, until one night, a few months later, I was watching TV with Angela. We had finally scrounged up enough money to get the TV fixed. It'd be a while before we could ever afford cable and subscribe to America's Number One Women's Television Network, but we were watching some late night news program, when I saw her. She was on a live segment that was just ending.

"Oh my God!" I slapped Angela's leg. "I had dinner with that woman! She was at that conference I went to in Washington."

"You're kidding me," Angela said. "You met *her*? Man, you really did hang with the high rollers."

"What do you mean? You know her?"

"Know her? Of course. Who doesn't know her?"

And it wasn't until the title bar came up on the screen and I saw the woman's name on the TV screen that it hit me. Of course! How could I not know who she was? She was no cokehead! Definitely not the woman I had made her out to be. And that endearing moniker? Most likely earned from some boarding school classmate or family member. How could I not know who this woman was? What an idiot I was, bailing on having dinner with her!

"Now, *she's* the ultimate contact for someone like you!" Angela gushed. "Man, so what did you talk about with her?"

And what could I do, but sink into the couch, as Angela turned up the volume?

"*. . . Reporting from the White House, this is Cokie Roberts, special correspondent.*"

Twentieth-Something Call

"Happy Holidays! Chavez residence."

"Hi, this is Michele Serros calling for Dr. Ernesto Chavez? Is he available?"

"Dr. Chavez is spending the Christmas holiday in Hawaii with his family. This is his housekeeper. May I take a message?"

"Do you know when he'll be back? I really need to talk to him."

"I believe sometime after January second, but then he's off to Miami to meet with the Cuban Cubic Zirconia Committee."

"Well . . . will you ask him to please call me?"

"Sure. Feliz Navidad!"

Fourth Thursday in April

Unlike the reasons the Ms. Foundation give to initiate "Take Our Daughters to Work Day," my father didn't take me to work so I could simply "celebrate my worth as a girl" or "gain confidence and voice in my opinions." No, my father's decision to let me accompany him to his job—that is, the one he held during the day—was simple: my parents couldn't afford a sitter. Great-Aunt Lydia announced she was fed up with all the grand-kids tearing the plastic off her living-room furniture, and unlike what so many people think of Mexican grandmothers, ours really disliked children. And for me to stay home? Now, that was out of the question, especially after that tortilla-frying incident I ignited in the kitchen last month. No, on my school's staff development day, it was decided I would go to work with my father.

While Patty Romero's dad sold gold anklet charms over the phone and Margaret Simon's dad actually drove over The Grade to work in Hollywood, it was my father who I believed had the most glamorous of all jobs. He worked in an atmosphere filled with movers and shakers, politicians, and deal makers, a place where foreign destination was the focus of everyone's personal and professional agenda. My father was a custodial engineer at the Oxnard City Airport.

He prepped me the night before about our father/daughter day together. "So, you know we're gonna have to get up early."

"Early like six?" I asked.

"No."

"Five?"

"Try more like four." He laughed.

"Four in the morning?" I cried. "Why so early?"

" 'Cause that's my job," he answered.

I started the day with my father, bleary-eyed and hungry. But the thought of eating was out of the question. It was just way too early. Once at the airport my father bought me a cup of hot water and opened a pack of powdered cocoa over it. As I sipped the hot chocolate I slowly began to feel more awake and alert. I followed him on his route around the airport terminal, helping him collect soiled papers, empty french-fry containers, and bits of chewing-gum foil from the ground. Inside the terminal I counted, one by one, the squares of tile that he buffed to a super-shiny gloss.

"Hey," I asked. "Did you know that you've cleaned nine hundred and twenty-eight squares so far?"

"So far?" he asked as he wiped his forehead. "It feels like a million."

I handed my father sheets of paper towels as he sprayed ammonia and water onto the large bay windows that overlooked the runway. From where we worked, we watched small planes whisk away families to exciting vacations outside of Oxnard.

"What kind of plane is that one?" I asked, pointing to a small aircraft with blue stripes.

"That's a Cessna," he answered. "Looks like a six-seater."

"Have you ever been in a plane like that?"

"No," my father said. "I hate planes."

Later I learned that everyone who headed toward the runway had to lay their luggage flat on its side on a conveyer belt. A monitor above the belt then exposed all the personal insides of the luggage. I stood at a distance anxiously hoping to snag a sight of some X-rayed brassieres or better yet, "chones." No such luck. I had fun guessing how many people would "go off" after walking through a metal archway and then watching one man, who refused to take off his belt buckle, start yelling and finally get taken away by security.

Yes, I felt proud knowing my father worked in such an interesting place, surrounded by worldly patrons, official-looking uniformed staff, and big-buckle-wearing madmen. Until a woman, at the reservations desk, asked me a question.

"Where are your parents, honey?" she asked. "You lost?"

"No, I'm here with my dad, George."

"George?" she responded with a surprised look. "Who's George?"

"George," I answered back. "He's my dad. You don't know who he is? He's been working here, like, forever."

I pointed out my father as he lugged a large gray waste bin out of the ladies' restroom.

"Oh," the woman remarked. "I've never noticed him before. Is he new?" She asked the man next to her, "Do you know any George?" The man shook his head.

I couldn't understand this woman's questions or the surprised tone in her voice. My father had worked a full three years at the airport, sweeping its floor, running feather dusters across its counters, dragging mops across the linoleum, and yet this woman, as well as the man next to her, my father's own coworkers, hadn't even heard of him.

Later that afternoon, on the way home, I skipped asking my father why his friends at work didn't know who he was. I guess, even at eleven years old, I knew the reason. It was as though he was a ghost, the brown ghost in green, unnoticed, not seen. I suddenly felt so ashamed of my father. I guess his job wasn't so glamorous after all.

Years later my father revealed something to me I never knew. He was awarded the Custodian III badge—a small, white, oval pin granted by executive personnel to janitors who exhibited a commitment to custodial engineering. But it was that pin, that small little pin, that scared my father. While janitorial work is a stable and honest way to make a living, and that pin represented a hefty raise, increasing his paycheck to a solid eighty dollars a week, it foreshadowed my father's future as a ghost; an invisible man no one would ever see, get to know, or, much less, respect.

For the past few years, during the month of April, I've read and heard about the millions of mothers, aunts, uncles, and fathers who've escorted their daughters, nieces, and young female friends to their own places of employment. I've seen the photos of *Time* magazine correspondents relate newsbreaking faxes to eight-year-old visitors. I've heard NPR commentators share airwaves with high-voiced preteens, and I read about the one girl whose father, a pilot, allowed her to request permission for takeoff from the cockpit of his very own plane.

Through this type of parental career guidance, this fourth Thursday in April declared "Take Your Daughters to Work Day," young girls are granted glimpses into their own futures, taught the benefits of career options available to them, and most importantly, how to value and respect a person's worth. But for me, this was a lesson learned too painfully.

Honor Thy Late-Night Phone Calls from Abuelita

It was a mid-Saturday afternoon and I was on the couch with Gabby Mi'jo, *again*. He and I were *always* on the couch. Locking lips, smacking hips, inhaling lengua. Fully clothed. We had yet to make the transition from living room to bedroom and it was driving me crazy.

"Aren't you getting tired of making out all the time?" I asked that afternoon.

"Why, are you?" he asked back.

"No, I just thought maybe you were."

"Why would I?"

"I just wanna make sure you're having fun."

"Isn't this fun for you?"

"I didn't say that. I just thought there might be something else you'd rather do."

"Like what? You wanna go to Tito's?" he suggested.

"No . . ."

"What, you want pizza?"

"Gabby, never mind. I'm sorry I even brought it up."

"Brought *what* up?"

This is how the couch conversations went. So frustrating that I'd just shove my tongue back in his mouth to stop the whole dialogue and we'd continue to make out, neither one of us initiating anything further.

Gabby Mi'jo was far from being boyfriend material. He was carless, directionless, bought all his sneakers from Payless, but me? I could care less. So why would I spend hundreds of afternoons with him on my lumpy couch, fully clothed and sharing spit when I could've been, say, alphabetizing my records or picking the pills off my angora sweater? Why? Because Gabby was a *fan.* How many women can say that? I fantasized casual introductions at future social functions.

"This is my father, George, my roommate, Angela, and, oh him? That's Gabby, he's my fan. For how long? Oh, I'd say for the last ten years of my career."

Gabby Mi'jo contacted me the way most fans do. Not by e-mail, not by calling the publicist in New York, not by sending a letter to my post office box, but by way of Grandma Soco. Grandma Soco is the lone female survivor of the family name. The family name that goes back to Mexico. Yes, *that* family name. While los privados in my family have opted for unlisted in the phone book, and the women, well, they've gone hyphenated or forfeited our paternal namesake for matrimonial assimilation, Grandma Soco is still a badge-bragging Serros, listed in the white pages alongside Grandpa Louie, who's been dead for over eighteen years. Gabby Mi'jo knew I was from Oxnard and on a whim called the first and only Serros he was given when he called directory assistance. That Serros was Grandma Soco. She didn't give him my number. She gave him my home address.

"Grandma," I asked, "why'd you give this guy my home address? That's more unsafe than giving out a phone number. Please don't do it again."

"Oh, but he sounded so nice," she said.

"Nice? Grandma, now how could you tell that?"

"He sounded Mexican."

When I finally got Gabby Mi'jo's letter, I opened it anxiously. It wasn't every day I got fan mail and his looked adorable. Sloppy handwriting on a black-and-white checkered envelope you just know he's had since the eighties. Inside, the typical misspelling of my first name:

"Dear Michelle," the letter started. "You don't know me. My name is Gabriel Morales and I'm a sales associate at SuperCrown Books . . ."

The rest was a blur of words linked together, but what stood out was, "I'm your biggest fan." Hmmm . . . a fan, eh? Friends, lovers, they come and go, but fans, you got them for life. Gabby Mi'jo included his phone number and I looked at the clock on my nightstand: 11:30 P.M. Well, he could've still been up. Is it rude to call someone you really don't know so late in the evening? Maybe. But he *was*, after all, a fan. He shouldn't mind. I immediately punched in his number.

A woman answered the phone. *Shit.* Girlfriend? Wife? I was about to hang up but instead I found myself asking for him. The woman covered the mouthpiece and called out, "Gaaa-beeee! Meeee-ho!" It was obviously his mother. Could it be he . . . *still lived at home?* The volume on the TV in the background was loud and I could tell *M*A*S*H* was just starting. God, I've always hated that song. She had to call out for him again. "Gaaa-beee, Meee-ho!"

"I'm so sorry," she apologized once she got back on the phone. "He just got home from work and he's got that TV of his blasting. Here, let me go get him for you."

I imagined her walking down a wood-paneled hallway covered with Sears family photos in thin cheap metal frames and maybe one of those cloth calendars depicting Columbus's discovery of America. Typical Mexican-American interior design found in the homes of many of my own relatives. It was all so familiar and endearing to me.

Over the blare of the TV I heard her say, "Mi'jo, someone's on the phone for you. I don't know. A girl."

"This is Gabby," he said once he got on the phone. His voice was nasally and after just five minutes of talking with him, I could detect the ten-year age difference between us. He was young, Mexican, and a fan. It was then I fell hard for this Gabriel Morales. The fan I hadn't even met. Could it get any better?

But as I found out, it didn't get better. He just wouldn't do it. Sleep with me, that is. He dug couch action.

"Maybe we should just go get those tacos at Tito's," I suggested out of mere frustration.

"Aren't you having fun?" He pulled one of the pills from my angora sweater out of his mouth.

"It's just we've been doing the same thing for so long," I complained. "The same ol' thing; don't you wanna try something new?"

"What, you wanna try their enchiladas?"

Now, normally, I wouldn't be after someone so heavily, but okay, I'll be honest. Things hadn't been going well. I was unhappy. My writing was beginning to suck. The little audiences in the coffeehouses were dwindling and the stories weren't coming like they used to. So, if I could at least get some action, some minor attention for some little thing I wrote a few years ago, well, why not? But *I* certainly didn't want to be the one to initiate that Gabby Mi'jo and I sleep together. I mean, I have my own pride, and suppose he tells people?

"Yeah, that poet chick was busting moves all over me, but I turned her ass down."

Qué embarrassing!

If only Gabby would unleash and unzip his inhibitions, I knew things could take place naturally. So, what would it take to make someone like him, the ardent admirer, and someone like me, let's say, the fancied one, to get a groove going?

Then I thought of it. Something he just couldn't resist. I reread his letter to reassure myself. His words, "I'm your biggest fan" stuck out like a billboard on Sunset Boulevard. This would be cake. And just in time. The springs from the couch were leaving welts on my backside.

"*You* know," I whispered to Gabby Mi'jo the next afternoon we were together. "I wrote a poem."

"*Hmmm, mmmm,*" he answered softly.

I brushed the hair out of my face and lowered my eyes. "I wrote a poem," I repeated. "About you."

"About *me*?" He immediately pulled back and opened his eyes.

"Yeah," I whispered.

"What did you write?" he asked.

"You know, just how great you are."

He sat up. "Are you serious?"

"Hmmm, mmmm . . ." I closed my eyes and kissed his ear.

"A poem about me." He looked up toward the ceiling. "Wow. You don't even know . . . this is like a dream, to have something about me in a book. I mean, I'm surrounded by books every day, but here, now, to be in one. Wow."

It had obviously made the impression I wanted.

"How many revisions have you done?"

"Um, so far? About eighteen." *Eighteen?*

"Eighteen?" he exclaimed. "Oh, my God, you only did five revisions on 'Masa on La Mesa' and that won the Vikki Carr Creative Writing Competition!"

"How did you know that?"

"Uh, you told me. Man," he repeated. "You must be getting it ready for publication! Are you? Is my poem gonna be in your next book?"

I looked into his brown eyes and, oh God, were his lashes always so black and beautiful? I just couldn't let him down. And the more questions he asked, the more I panicked. The truth was I hadn't written a poem, a sentence, a word, anything about Gabby Mi'jo. I just took the chance that feeling immortalized in a poem would make him glow, make him excited, and that alone would make him want to create a deeper bond with me.

"Well, I was thinking about it. I mean, I want *it in,*" trying to give him subliminal messages. "I've already told my editor about it."

"You told your editor?" He started to unbutton his shirt. "About me?"

"Well, yeah," I purred.

"Oh, Michele, I think it's so *hot* you wanna have a poem about me in your book." He moaned softly and brought his lips back to my neck. His fingers locked around mine. He took my hand and led me to my bedroom.

Finally.

* * *

The next evening I got a call from Gabby Mi'jo. It was a little after eleven P.M. and he just got off work.

"Hey," he bragged. "I put your book on the staff recommendation shelf."

"Really? Oh Gabby, that's so sweet."

"Yeah, I sorta got into a fight with my coworker. He wanted to keep Tom Clancy on. But you know, I gotta take care of my baby."

This was twice as good!

"So, what did you do today?" he continued.

"Oh, I cut down old band flyers for scrap paper and then—"

"Did you work on the poem?" he interrupted.

"Poem?"

"The poem you wrote for me."

"Oh, yeah, well, actually I looked it over. Yeah."

"It's not one of those short Japanese poems, is it?"

"You mean a haiku?"

"Yeah. No wait, I take that back. I mean, I don't mind if it is. Really, I don't even know why I said that. I just wonder what you wrote."

"Oh, don't worry. You're gonna like it."

"So, when can I see it?"

"Gabby, it's not that simple. I mean, sometimes I get nervous sharing some of my work. Specially pieces that are so personal."

"It's personal? How personal? Oh, hey, *M*A*S*H* is starting. Why don't you watch it and I'll watch it and it'll be like we're watching it together but at separate houses?"

"Oh, Gabby, *you* are the most romantic boy in the world."

I've always felt like a loser lying around in bed in the middle of the afternoon, but with Gabby Mi'jo it was so different. It was three P.M. and we were still under the covers looking up at the faded glow-in-the-dark star stickers on my ceiling. I had an after-sex snack on my mind when he asked, "So, what did you write about me?"

"Whaddya mean?" I looked over at him.

"In my poem. What did you say?"

"Oh, you know . . ." My voice trailed off. What could I say? *I* didn't even know.

"I feel like . . ." Gabby Mi'jo started. "What's it called when someone or something makes an artist think of something?"

"A source of inspiration?"

"No, that word, it sounds like mucus."

"Muse?"

"Yeah, that's it. So am I, like, your muse?" He smiled slowly and I saw his chipped tooth.

"You know"—I smiled back—"I think you are."

"And I think," he said, pulling the covers over him and getting on top of me, "that I can be late for work."

I never had so much of Gabby Mi'jo that month. Why hadn't I thought of the poem thing earlier? Talk of the poem worked like foreplay.

"So have you picked out a title?" he whispered.

"Sorta," I whispered back.

"That's usually the hardest part, huh? Coming up with a title."

"Hmmm, mmmm," I agreed, unzipping his painter pants. "It's *very* hard."

"So, how many stanzas are in it?" he moaned.

"So far six."

"Six? My, that's a lot of words for little ol' me."

"You're far from little, *Gabriel*."

* * *

But by the third month the honeymoon was over. Gabby Mi'jo didn't want to have any more sex with me till he saw the poem.

"I don't think you really wrote a poem about me," he snapped suspiciously.

"Gabby, of course I did. Why would I tell you that?"

"I dunno, I just think it's weird that it's been over two months and I haven't seen this poem."

"Oh Gabby, wouldn't you rather wait and see it published? Won't that be better, more fun?" I started to undo his belt buckle.

"So when is this book coming out?"

"Uh, I'm not really sure."

He pushed my hand away. "I gotta go."

"Gabby, baby, wait. What's up?"

"Nothing." He fastened his belt buckle. "It's just that my mom's making Frito pie tonight and I'm already late for dinner."

I had to write the poem. Any poem. But what could I possibly write? What could I possibly say about Gabby Mi'jo? He was making it all so difficult, making such a production out of nothing. Men, they always gotta have their little dance of courtship.

I spent the following week trying to come up with something. His looks, his voice, the cute little mature way he answers the phone at work: "SuperCrown Books. This is Gabriel speaking. How can I help you?" *Sigh*.

Something, anything would do, but nothing was coming to me. I rhymed, did exercises. Gabby, fabby . . . cabby . . . ugh. I went to the library to search for inspiration. Finally in the foreign literature section, I found this one book. A hardcover book of poetry from the late seventies by this poet named Eva Perez. Her name sounded so familiar, but I just couldn't remember where I'd heard of her. Anyway, she was from Peru and she had this short poem about some long-distance lover. It was exactly six stanzas. It was perfect. It was beautiful. It would do the trick. I checked the book out, feeling smug that I could have her poem rewritten, à la me, by that evening, which meant I could have sex with Gabby Mi'jo before his shift the next day.

The next morning I looked over the Eva Perez poem. It was now restyled and retitled on a piece of my personal stationery with my signature. I called Gabby Mi'jo right away.

"You wanna come over later?" I asked.

"I dunno," he answered dryly. "My dad needs help in the garage."

"Well, when you're done maybe you can stop by. I wanna show you your poem. It's done."

"It is? I'll catch the number six right over."

Gabby Mi'jo was over in twenty-five minutes.

"So, can I see the poem?" he asked through the screen door.

"Dang, Gabby." I took his hand and let him in. "It's been so long since I've seen you. First let's have some fun. Mind if we just kick it in the bedroom for a while?"

"Well, okay. But then I wanna see the poem."

Twenty minutes later we were both looking up at the stars on the ceiling, sweaty and breathing hard. "You know, Gabby," I started. "I'm thinking of using a different font just for your poem, different than the rest of the poems in the book."

"Really? Wow."

I leaned over to my nightstand, opened the drawer, and pulled out the poem.

"Okay, now." I held the paper over my chest. "Be kind. I put a lot of time and emotion into this."

"Just let me see it already!" He laughed and grabbed the paper from me. He looked it over.

"So, when did you finish this?" he asked.

"Oh Gabby, baby." I stretched under the covers and pulled them up to my chest. "I don't think it'll ever be finished." I leaned over and kissed the side of his neck. "It's an ongoing labor of love. An epic. I think the longer *we're* together, the longer the poem will ultimately be. The more intense *we* are, the more intense it will be. You know what I mean?"

He read it over again. "So, you wrote this?"

"Gabby, of course I wrote it." I pulled the covers closer to my face. "Oh, you're thinking 'cause my voice, the way I wrote it, is different from other things I've written?"

"I know what 'voice' means," he snapped.

"But, baby, it's just you're so unique and I had to go with what my muse gives me." I started twirling the hairs on his chest. "Don't you like it?"

He didn't answer. He just kept looking over the poem.

"So, you obviously know who Eva Perez is," he said slowly.

"Eva who?" I answered in a confused tone.

He held up the poem and looked at me sideways. "Michele, this is her poem."

"What?"

"Come on, Michele, I work at SuperCrown. Or did you forget? This poem is an Eva Perez poem, you just moved a few words around."

"Gabby . . ."

He got up from the bed and grabbed his pants from the floor. "You lied to me!"

"Wait . . ."

He started pulling his pants on and pulled his white T-shirt over his chest. He grabbed his car keys off the nightstand.

"Gabby, no," I begged. "Please, don't go. Let me explain."

But it was too late; he was already leaving the bedroom and storming down the hallway.

"Wait!" I called out. "Gabby, wait! I'm thinking of writing a novel and you're gonna be the protagonist. The *main* character!"

I never heard from Gabby Mi'jo again. Every time I called, his mother told me in an uncomfortable tone that he wasn't home even though I could hear his TV in the background.

And I could have written it off. I mean, using poetry for sex, taking advantage of a sales associate at SuperCrown. But it was so painful and I missed Gabby Mi'jo so much. Lying on the couch just to watch TV became pathetic and I cried uncontrollably every time our song, the theme for *M*A*S*H,* came on.

I longed to hear from Gabby Mi'jo once more. I searched the far back end of my mailbox, asked the publicist in New York, and checked my e-mail. Nothing. Gabby Mi'jo disappeared from my life as quickly as he entered it. Then one day, during the afternoon, I decided to visit him at work. I guess I just wanted to *feel* near him. I saw his picture hanging behind the cash register and learned that he had made Employee of the Month. The words "Assistant Manager in Training" were underneath his smiling face and I couldn't remember him looking so happy. He was obviously doing well without me. As I was about to leave the store, I saw three books by Eva Perez on the staff recommendation shelf. I found my own book marked down, way down, and placed on a table alongside bookmarkers and last year's calendars. I burst into tears and immediately left the store.

And while I was sad and all, I couldn't help but think what a selfish idiot I had been. I mean Gabby Mi'jo was a person. A lover of literature, a boy who helped his dad in the garage, a fan of my poetry, and here I just used him for my own hormonal needs and to pump my flagging self-esteem. Do you think Maya Angelou uses poetry to lure potential play? Does Robert Pinsky have a Rolodex of sexual conquests? Do Pulitzer Prize winners hand out copies of their hotel keys at book signings? Most positively not. I was a horrible, horrible poet person.

That night the phone rang. I looked at my clock and saw it was a little after eleven P.M. Could it possibly be . . . Gabby Mi'jo, just getting off his shift? Perhaps someone from his work recognized me from my earlier visit and they told him and now he had a change of heart. Oh, it couldn't be him, could it?

I answered the phone and I was right. It wasn't him. It was Grandma Soco.

"Ay, mi'ja." She clicked her tongue. "I'm so sorry to be calling so late."

"No, it's not too late, Grandma," I answered halfheartedly. "What's wrong?"

"Well, this boy called here wanting to get ahold of you and I remembered what you told me about not giving out information about you. But oh, he was so nice. A real nice Mexican boy."

"Grandma." My heart raced and my hopes rose. "Was his name Gabby Mi'—I mean, was his name Gabriel?"

"No, no, it wasn't."

My heart sank.

"And," she continued proudly, "even though he insisted he was your biggest fan, I didn't give him any information about you. Nothing, nada. Just like you asked me."

My heart sank deeper.

Here was a fan, a boy. A nice Mexican boy and the opportunity was lost. Thanks a friggin' lot, Grandma Soco!

"No, what I did this time," she said, "was get *his* number."

I looked at the clock on my nightstand. 11:09 P.M. "Quick, Grandma," I said as I searched for a pen in the nightstand drawer. "Give me his number, quick."

Good Parking

A scholarship and a house. That's what it took for me to finally ask my father to visit. In the ten years of living in Los Angeles, my father has never visited me, not once. I've never invited him. I guess I always wanted to be in a living situation he would be proud of and now I was living in a house. Small, but still a house and I had just won a university scholarship. This would be a perfect time. He would be impressed and I was definitely ready for him.

So I called my old baby-sitter, Connie, who still lives in El Rio, right next door to him. I didn't call her to tell her about the award or to ask her to make the trip to L.A. with him. No, I needed her to walk over to my father's house and ask him to call me. My father doesn't have a phone. He always says, "If someone really wants to tell me something they can write me a letter. Why should *I* pay for what *they* want to say?" So Connie is his only connection to the outside world. When she goes over to tell him someone needs to talk to him, he walks over to El Rio Stop & Shop and makes the call, the length of his conversation depending on how many dimes he has in his pocket.

About an hour later I got his phone call.

"Why are you telling Connie our business?" my father accused me.

"Dad, all I did was ask her to ask you to call me. I don't have a choice 'cause you don't have a phone."

"Well . . ." He relaxed a bit. "What do you need?"

I tell him about the scholarship. I tell him how I want him to go to the awards ceremony with me. "But," I tell him, "it's from six-thirty to seven-thirty . . . at night."

My father goes to bed at seven P.M. every night. If he were to come to the ceremony with me, we wouldn't be getting off the UCLA campus till almost eight and then there's the one-hour drive back to Oxnard. He wouldn't be getting to bed till after nine P.M. and I don't think he's done that since high school.

But his response really surprised me. "Oh, that's no problem," he said. "I'll be there. But I'm gonna get to your house early. I'm gonna get there early so we can find good parking."

To my father, good parking means free parking. I grew up being driven in circles around city blocks all in the name of good parking. As my sister and I grew nauseated in the backseat of his VW, my father would claim, "The city doesn't deserve more money than it already has."

My father arrived at my house at two P.M., four and a half hours before the ceremony. I met him at the door in cutoffs and a sweatshirt.

"What?" he asked when he saw me through the screen door. "You're not even ready?"

"Dad," I said as I started to let him in, "it's not until tonight. Why are you here so early?"

"Oh, you think this is early, but let me tell you, time, it goes by like *that*." He snapped his fingers. "Remember when you were just in high school and having all that trouble, and I said it would all pass. 'Blink your eyes and it's gonna pass before you know it.' Well, didn't it? Didn't it all pass?"

"Dad, those were the longest four years of my life." I cleared off the couch so he could sit down, but he wasn't listening. He was now going through my records.

"Hey, is this a Ritchie Valens album?"

"Yeah," I told him. "You wanna hear it?"

"Oh, I love Ritchie Valens! You know he was from La Colonia?"

"Dad, you think everyone is from Colonia. He was from *Pacoima,* not Colonia."

"He was? Are you serious? Man, all this time . . . well, yeah, put it on and then you can go get ready and then we can go out and get a soda or something."

To my father "a soda or something" means a soda and . . . nothing else. My father hates eating out. To him, restaurants are a big waste of time and money. "You know why they always bring you a salad?" he asks all the time. "To fill you up. All that lettuce has water on it and anyone knows water fills you up right away and then they bring you just a little piece of meat and you can't even enjoy that 'cause you're so full from all the water. Hey, you know Bobby? Well, his daughter went to Italy. And you know what? Over there they serve the salads *after* your food and they're small and you don't even have to eat it."

I went to my room while my dad sang along to "Donna" . . . *I had a girl and Donna was her name* . . . He looked out the front window, swaying his head slowly and shaking the change in his pocket. I wondered if this one song was reviving a whole high-school experience for him. He suddenly looked sad. Did he have a girl named Donna? He should've just blinked *his* eyes to make it all pass.

I went through my closet and thought how it was going to be a long night. He hadn't even congratulated me, nothing about my award or anything. Maybe if we saw a movie it would kill some time and I would stop feeling sorry for myself.

"Hey, Dad," I called from my bedroom. "Do you wanna go see *Mi Familia*? We can still see it on a big screen."

"Is that that movie with that guy from *L.A. Law*?" he asks.

"Yeah, Jimmy Smits."

"Nah, I don't like him. I don't like all that Mexican gang stuff. I grew up with it. Why should I have to pay to see it all over again?"

"Dad, *Mi Familia*'s not about gangs," I told him, "It's about family life, a Mexican family, like ours."

"Then why should I pay to see that? I already know about that. People should pay me. What about *Congo*? Is that out yet?"

I came out of my bedroom and found my father looking around the kitchen. I was getting annoyed. "Forget a movie," I told him. "So I guess we'll just get that soda or something."

"What's this?" he asked, looking at the kitchen counter.

"Oh, that's a tortilla maker," I told him.

"A tortilla maker! Are you serious? You're kidding, right? You were born with a tortilla maker, like this!" He slapped his palms together quickly back and forth, like he really had a piece of masa between them. "I can't believe you actually spent money on something like this. God, I'm so happy your mother isn't alive to see this!"

"Dad," I told him, "who has time to make tortillas by hand? This thing only takes seconds." I pulled it out from the counter to show him but he wasn't listening, he was back in the living room.

"So, Michele, do you own this place or are you still renting?"

"Own! Dad, how could I possibly own a house in the middle of L.A.? I'm still a student. I can barely work part-time. Do you know how much a place like this is worth with the property and the garage and the great street parking."

"Street parking? You pay extra to park on the street? In El Rio, everyone parks for free. You know, you'll never be able to buy a house if you keep giving your money away to the city to park on its street."

I was feeling more and more like a failure. Why did I ask him to visit? I was not ready for this. I was not ready for him. I was twenty-seven years old. When my father was twenty-seven, he was a married man and the father of two. At age twenty-seven he held the keys to a brand-new car and a custom home he not only built, but owned. At age twenty-seven, my father's credit could buy him the world. He would never understand where I was in life.

I grabbed my bag and opened the front door. "Let's just go," I told him.

We walked down my walkway and were getting into my car when he asked, "So hey, how much is this scholarship for?"

"It's for three thousand dollars." Suddenly the amount seemed like nothing.

"Three thousand? Now, that's a nice chunk of money. What did you have to do?"

"Oh, write this essay," I told him. Why was he even asking?

"Three thousand dollars? For an essay? Are you serious? So how long did it take you?"

"I dunno, about four hours . . . I mean, after editing and everything," I told him.

Uh-oh, I thought, here it comes. Now he was gonna tell me what I could have been doing in those four hours, how in those four hours I could have been studying, or looking for a better job, or how four hours is a lot of time to gamble for an award I may not have won.

"Do you know how long it took me to make three thousand dollars when I was your age? Do you know how long I had to drag that mop across the linoleum at the Oxnard airport? When I was your age I couldn't even dream of having three thousand dollars all to myself. You know, money like that doesn't come easy. That's the problem with a lot of kids, they don't know the meaning of hard work. They just write an essay and then they get three thousand dollars."

My father pulled out his wallet and flipped through it. "You know," he said as his voice softened a bit, "I didn't realize you had won so much money. We should really celebrate better."

I couldn't believe it. Through the corner of my eye I saw him look through his wallet again. I could see a thick tight wad of green bills.

"Three thousand dollars, huh?" he asked again. "That's almost a thousand bucks an hour! You're doing pretty good." He paused. "You know what? Forget about getting just a soda. We're gonna go get something to *eat*. We're gonna go to a restaurant! And you know"—he thumbed through his money again—"I'm gonna let *you* pay."

Mind Your Table Manners

They're usually card tables. Pretty sturdy ones actually, that some part-time clerk pulls out from the back closet, sets up, and tops with a small vase of gerbera daisies. If you're Mexican, they'll cover the table with that festive-looking oilcloth your grandma picks up for a buck fifty a sheet, but they'll brag that they "found" it for a mere nine bucks a yard over at some ethnic specialty store. The cloth makes you feel safe. Everybody knows that there's no place warmer and more comfy than a Mexican grandmother's kitchen. You instantly feel weepy. But whatever you do, hold back your tears (see Role Model Rule Number 4).

Someone from the store's staff will offer you a glass of wine, red or white. "We got a shitload of this Peter Vella left over from when Greg Louganis was here," they'll say. "Would you care to have some?" If you're like me, you'll skip the vino and request a Loco Half 'n Half, which is my favorite drink from Pollo Loco—

half Horchata Olé and half Piña Colada Bang. If you're guaranteed to sell more than five books, they'll get anything for you.

This is the gravy, the niceties, I call them, of your actual book signing. Months earlier the foundation had already been set; you've confirmed the time and date, sent out all the flyers, faxed announcements to the weeklies, and now you're actually peeking out from the two-way "spy on deadbeat employee" mirror of the store manager's office, praying that interested book-type people, or even a few English students looking for class credit, will show up. Then, slowly, you witness a small crowd beginning to form. They start to fill up the seats. You check your watch and know better than to start on time. You wait the obligatory fifteen minutes. The assistant manager of the bookstore welcomes the crowd and reads a list of upcoming in-store events. The crowd oohs and aahs. You wonder if they oohed and aahed when your reading was mentioned a few weeks earlier. Then she finally announces your presentation, performance, reading, whatever, and suddenly you get nervous. Will people really believe that's a mere cold sore on your lip and not a herpes "cochina" scab, as Cousin Benny calls them? You look down and see the red polish on your toenails is chipped, exposing the green underneath. Your feet scream Christmas and here it is mid-March. Too late for any touch-ups. You hear a damp applause and that's your cue. You appear from the manager's office and quickly hide behind the podium to camouflage your stomach. You don't think someone made a trip to Pollo Loco and came back with only a beverage, do you? You smile, exhale, and acknowledge the adoring faces.

"*Thank* you. Thank you," you say. "Oh, it's wonderful to see so many people here!" *There could be more. What's up with these empty chairs in the front? You specifically told the manager you wanted a minimal amount of chairs so that more people would have to stand and then it would look crowded and then you'd feel more in demand and then . . . okay, stop it, you're beginning to sound like Diana Ross in* Mahogany*!*

"It's so great to be back in L.A.!" *Is it really? You like to get out of this fake-ass town as much as possible and now you're being fake just by claiming it's great to be back. You've really just come back from visiting Auntie Berta in that stinky nursing facility in Fontana, but they don't need to know that. Let them think you've been on tour, on the East Coast, in New York. Yeah.*

"I'd like to start off with something a little different." *Different than what? And why? They don't know what you usually read. Are you trying to make them feel special? Oh, your special little reading for your special little audience, so little they didn't even FILL UP ALL THE CHAIRS! Okay, just read something from your book already!*

And so you start sharing stories and you talk and read words that you've chosen for the next forty-five minutes or so and then you finally say, "Thank you very much," and that's the audience's cue to clap. You hear what sounds like another round of damp applause and then you take your drink, you take your book, and you're led to The Table, that card table where you'll meet a small percentage of people from the audience, people who actually bought your book and want it signed. Now, this is the meat of your book signing. This is about sales. Profit. Percentage. Will you ever sell enough books to pay all your late fees at Hollywood Video? Enough royalties to get Sallie Mae off your back? The more you smile, the more people will like you and want to buy another copy of your book, so you have to be nice and smile. A lot.

Now, many discussions occur at The Table and you must remain pleasant and cheerful at all times.

* * *

The first person is a woman. I open her book and I see my signature already written across the bottom of the second page.

"Oh," I point out, "I've already signed it."

"Yes, you signed it," she says firmly. "But not the way I wanted."

"What? I mean, excuse me?" I smile up at her.

"You don't remember me, do you?" she says. "I met you at Book Village in San Jose about a month ago and I specifically said to write something about my daughter getting married and you didn't."

"Well, it does say 'congratulations.' " I point out the under-lined inscription.

"Yes, it says congratulations. But for what? My daughter has had many achievements in her life. How is she gonna remember which one you're talking about? Sure she hasn't written a book, yet, but how is she gonna know what you're congratulating her for? Just rewrite it, would you?"

I smile and write in "on your upcoming nuptials" to the already existing "congratulations."

The woman takes the book back. "No, she's already gotten married! Jesus, can't you fix it?"

I cross out "upcoming" and add "marriage—it's not for the pregnant anymore!" The page is marked up with the blue ink corrections and additions.

"You know," the woman says as she hovers over me. "I really should just get another one."

"Oh, you wanna buy another book?" I eye the store's cashier.

"*Buy* one? I shouldn't have to pay for it. After all, it was you who made the mistake."

She then grabs the book back and leaves The Table before I can really say anything. I remind myself to find out if she paid by check so I can copy down her phone number and prank-call her later. Then I remember she had bought the book a month ago. Damn!

The next person is a young thin blond woman with brown lipstick and black polyester pants.

"Hi." I smile up at her. "Who should I sign this for?"

"Oh, just your name will do." She waves her hand carelessly in the air. "So, hey, have you thought of the talent for the feature?"

"Talent?"

"Like, I can totally see Andy Garcia as your brother and definitely Edward James Olmos as your Mexican dad."

"My Mexican dad?"

"Yeah. You know." She then leans into The Table. "I saw *American Me* twice."

Yeah, and I saw Deliverance *once.*

"Yeah, Edward James Olmos would make a great Mexican dad. Wouldn't he?" I smile.

𝓑𝓮𝓱𝓲𝓷𝓭 the aspiring casting agent is a young guy. He isn't holding a copy of my book, but actually a copy of another book. He places it casually on The Table.

"This is my book," he announces.

"Your book?" I open it and look over a few pages. "Wow, congratulations."

"Yeah." He underlines his name, Marco De Valle, on the cover with his finger. "This is me . . . You've never heard of me? Mine's in *hardcover*."

"Uh, not really, but you know I'm really behind with my reading and there's a lot out there."

"Yeah," he agrees. "A lot of *shit*. But you know . . ." And then his voice lowers. "I haven't sold that many copies and I'm wondering, well, I was just wondering how you think I can get the word out."

"Well," I tell him. "You're gonna have to do a ton of readings, put stuff on the Internet, start personal mailing lists, visit schools, cut ribbons at Latino-owned skateboard parks—" I know he isn't really listening to me.

"Man, that's a lot of work," he interrupts.

"Yeah, but if you want your book to sell—"

"That's too much work. I don't wanna have to do all that. I just wanna write."

Well, don't we all? "So, did you want me to sign your book?" I smile at him.

"You mean *my* book?"

"No, I mean, one of my books. You want me to sign it?"

"Nah, I mean, I didn't buy one."

"Oh, well, is this for me?" I looked at the book he's written. *Oh, I'm gonna take it back and get me some store credit, maybe get the new Frank Black CD.*

"Oh, no." He takes it from my hands and puts it back in his backpack. "I just wanted you to see it."

"Oh, well, thank you for your support!" I call out to him as he leaves the line.

Next is a young girl and her mother.

"This is the first time my daughter has ever attended a live reading," the mother gushes. "This is the first time she's actually met an actual author."

"Oh, that's so nice." I smile at her daughter and soften my voice. "Hi there, what's your name?" The girl doesn't respond.

"She's really shy," the mother explains. "She never really talks. She just loves to read and read and read."

"Oh." I laugh. "Lucky for all the writers in the world." I take the book from the girl's hands. "So, who do I make this out to?"

"You can make it out to her," the mother says. "Her name's Ixotchltiquelta."

"E-ah . . . ?"

"Ixotchltiquelta," she repeats. "You've never heard it? It's a common name in the Nahuatl language."

"Oh, right." I attempt to write out the name as it sounded.

"Nooo." The woman looks at my handwriting and frowns. "*IX*, not *EX*, and there's only one *C*. No, not like that. No, *Q* not *G*. Oh forget it! Just put down Jenny. That's what her grandparents call her."

"Oh, I feel horrible," I tell the mother. "I really butchered her name."

"Well, that's okay," she responds halfheartedly. "She's used to it. You don't write or read Nahuatl?"

"No, not really."

The mother clicks her tongue and remarks, "That's really a shame."

"Do you?"

"I'm starting. I'm taking lessons over at the Learning Annex."

I continue my dedication and I rub an itch on the side of my nose. Suddenly I feel something loosen and I grow anxious. How am I gonna take care of something in my nose without everyone thinking I have some weird tick or perhaps a drug problem? (see Role Model Rule Number 10). I look down on the page and am horrified to see a small dry something or another has fallen from the inside of my nose and is now in the middle of the page. Is it really green or just a reflection from the fluorescent lighting? I don't know if I should look up and check if the girl and her mother have seen it or if I should just nonchalantly brush it away and keep writing? Should I circle the snot, slam the book shut, and deem it performance art?

But I don't do any of those things and instead, I just date my signature and give them back the book.

"Oh, thank you," the mother continues to gush. "This was pleasant. Thank you!"

Whew! They didn't see my booger fall. They both walk away and I overhear the mother remark, "Isn't that nice, Ixotchlti-quelta? You got your book signed by an actual author!"

"But, Mom"—I hear the young girl suddenly speak up—"Her *booger's* in it. I don't want her ol' snot in my book!"

The mother grabs the girl's arm. "Shhhh! It'll be worth more when she dies."

Faces, people, and smiles, one by one. Everyone wanted their own words in my handwriting. Women seeking advice how to improve their writing and men asking how to publish manuscripts they hadn't even started to write. It's the same situation in every city, every county. And then I see *him.*

I looked up and right there in front of me, on the other side of The Table, is the most heavenly face I've seen in a long time. He's a twenty-something tall thing, a Mexican, a naturally *red-headed* Mexican, you know the kind with dark red layers of thick hair, a copper complexion, and a dab of light brown freckles across the nose? My favorite.

"Hiya," he said.

Hiya? Suddenly it's the sweetest salutation I've ever heard. So goony *Hee Haw* cute. I smiled to myself.

"Oh, these are for you."

He brought me flowers!

I stood up. I felt my skirt's waistband pinching me. Damn,

why did I polish off that whole Pollo Bowl? "Oh, they're so beautiful." *Thank God, no baby's breath.* This guy is perfect.

"You know, you're my favorite Chicana author."

"Really?" I giggled. "Oh, you must not read a whole lot." Now, normally I would've been offended. What's up with the marginalization, dude? Like *My Favorite Martian?* An alien? What's that supposed to mean? But instead I just smiled more.

"No, I mean it," he insisted. "I drove over an hour to get here."

I couldn't even look at him. I covered my cold sore with one hand and started to sign his book. I tried to focus and steady my shaking hands. God, I was suddenly so nervous! His own hands were on The Table and he was tapping his keys on it. I checked the keys. Was one of them a hotel key? (see Role Model Rule Number 11.) Was it a message? A sexual Morse code in his tap, tap, tapping?

"So, what's your name?" I tried to sound casual and noticed my pen was also shaking.

"Xavier," he answered.

"With an X?" I asked. I couldn't stop smiling!

"Of course."

I'm designing wedding invitations in my mind.

"So, um, I was wondering . . ." Xavier the redheaded Mexican hesitated.

Oh, he's shy. I'm making him nervous. Just what was he wondering?

"Is there any way I can get a hold of you?"

Not that shy.

"I'm putting on a fund-raiser and I was hoping—" he continued.

"Oh, yes," I interrupted him. "I just love giving back to my community! Here." I jotted out my phone number in the book.

"There's my work number, my home number, my e-mail address, and the number of my grandma Soco."

"Grandma Soco?"

"She can get ahold of me no matter what," I explained.

"So." He looked at my numbers. "I'll give you a call this week."

"Yes, that'd be perfect." My voice suddenly became high and soft.

And then Xavier, who spells his name with an *X,* started to walk away. But then he turned around. What was this? One last comment? One last look into my eyes before his long lonely drive back home?

"Oh, by the way," he said, "I just loved your first book."

"My first book?" I asked, confused.

"Yeah, *The House on Mango Street.*"

The Plaintiff, the Poet

"Mr. Chavez, you seem like a reasonable man. And from what you tell me in your deposition, an upstanding citizen of your community. That's why I don't understand why you're even here. But let me ask you, Mr. Chavez, at this event, the event you had in . . . May of 1998, did you have caterers, servers, valet parkers?"

"Yes, of course, Your Honor."

"What about any floral arrangements? Did you have any gardeners come the day before to spiff up your yard? A pool man to clean your pool?"

"Well, yes."

"And, sir, did you pay them for their services?"

"Well, of course."

"So how is it, Mr. Chavez, that you would make a promise, a verbal contract with a poet to read at your event to, as you say in your deposition, 'add some cultural entertainment' to your

Wednesday Afternoon Latino Fine Arts League luncheon and then not pay that poet?"

"Well, I . . . I guess it wasn't a priority."

"It wasn't a priority?"

"Well, I mean . . ."

"I rule in favor of the plaintiff, the poet! Mr. Chavez, I order you to pay the twenty-five dollars owed to the poet, the twelve dollars and eighty cents she made in phone calls, and I'm adding an additional two thousand dollars for punitive damages."

"Two thousand dollars! Your Honor, don't you think that's a little extreme?"

"Mr. Chavez, I have to make an example out of you. I need to send a message to all the community members out there that I have no patience for this brown-on-brown crime. To cheat a poet out of monetary acknowledgment is the most pathetic act I've seen all my years on the bench. That's all I have to say to you. Next case, *The Performance Artist* v. *California Polytechnic State University*!"

Role Model Rule Number 13

Answer All Fan Mail

Dear Michele Serros,

Hello, I am an English teacher and bought a copy of your book at a local bookstore here in Calabasas. You have some very nice poems. You need to, however, concentrate on making your poems more universal. The average kid in Connecticut may not understand your stories and you need to make them accessible to everyone. Instead of using a colloquial term such as *chicharrones*, why not just pork or ham? A ham sandwich? Everyone knows what that is. Next time you sit down to write, think about the kid in Connecticut. Will he be able to appreciate and grasp what you are trying to say?

Poetry is a very difficult market to succeed in, so I offer you the best of luck. I myself have sent out manuscripts for the last ten *years and have yet to be published and I have a master's in creative writing.*

Sincerely,
Donald P. McWhite, M.A.

Dear Michele,

First of all I want to apologize for not returning your calls. I guess I was still upset with you about the poem thing. Your book just came into my store and it reminded me of you. I read a little bit of it when we aren't too busy, but I'm a store manager now, so I don't have much time. Anyway, if you're interested I'd like to have you here at SuperCrown for a book signing. You can call the store and ask for Lillian. She's the readings coordinator and sorta my girlfriend. So if you come, please don't mention we used to watch M*A*S*H together, if you know what I mean.

Gabriel J. Morales

Hey Michele,

Wow, I guess you did well at Columbia and everything. My mom bought me a copy of your book, thinking she remembered you from studying over here with me. I haven't read the book and the real reason why I'm writing is because I lost your number. I went to Alexander's but they wouldn't tell me your work schedule and I really want to know when the next "Friends of Employees" picture-frame sale is. Please call me.

Your friend,
Nikki Chase

Dear Michele,

Thank you for sending me your book. I will read it soon. I'm sure it's very nice. By the way, your parking tickets keep coming to the house. Please, mi'ja, READ the parking signs.

Dad

Dear Michael Hill,

Just joking! Hey it's me, Martha, Martha Reyes! I go by Marti now. Hey, what's up? It's been soooooo long since I've seen or talked to you. I ran into your grandma Soco over at Bob's, the one on Vineyard, and she gave me your address. I wanted your phone number but she was all tight with it. She said she can only give it to certain people. Well, anyway, I was in the B. Dalton bookstore over here in the Esplanade and saw your name on a book! I couldn't believe it! I told the cashier, "Hey, I know her! She was my best friend!" but that witch didn't even give me a discount. But that's life, in Oxnard anyway. I would like to see you sometime. Maybe if you're not too busy, you can come visit me.

Well, I just wanted to say hi and tell you I'm thinking of you and say that in the picture of you on your book, your clothes look real nice. Write me, 'kay?

Marti

Dear Ms. Ceros,

My mom just bought me your book and I have to say, I didn't want to read it, but when we got home, and I hope I'm not being rude, but on the second page of your book there was some dried booger, my mom says secretion, from your nose and we were going to remove it that same day we bought your book, but when my father was about to scrape it off he noticed it was in the shape, he calls it an aparishun, the shape was of one of Jesus' tears, like when he is on the cross already close to deth. My mother tore out the page with your booger on it and its in our living room in a shoe box and surrounded by cotton balls. It looks really pretty and a bunch of people from our neighborhood came to see it. And my aunt sells corn on the cob, my dad calls them elotays, for all the people that wait in line and my uncle met people who need some work done on their cars and my sister finally met a boy, he came with his sick grandma, to get healed, and me, well, I'm just writing to tell you that you are a very very good roll model and that page in your book has changed our lives more than you'll ever, ever know.

Love,
Ixotchltiquelta Hagen-Perez

P.S. Write back!

Special Assembly, Part 2

Fifteen after ten. Fifteen minutes and already all those kids, brown kids, inner-city low-income underprivileged children of under-represented ethnic minorities have been waiting in a cafeteria. Waiting for me, their woman, brown woman, suburban-raised, low on income, low on gas, from an underrepresented ethnic minority. And here I am late, again.

God, why didn't I check Angela's *Thomas Brother's Guide* last night? Why didn't I make sure I had enough gas in my tank *yesterday*? All these unplanned stops and pullovers make me late. And why, why did I have to make what I thought was gonna be a quick stop at Lupe's Panaderia for that café con leche? Okay, okay, so it wasn't a Panaderia. It was actually the Starbucks at Venice Crossroads and I got me a frappuccino. Gotta make sure I ditch the cup before I enter Bell Gardens. Don't wanna cross-contaminate, as Alex says. Uppity Westside trash belongs on the uppity Westside.

If I had done all this and skipped all that I would've already been there. Been on that pullout stage from the cafeteria wall, reading the paper-clipped pages I've been reading for the past two years now, retelling the same jokes, recounting the same memories. . . . *and then my English teacher told me, "You could never be a writer . . ."*

But instead I am God knows where, fifteen minutes late, and . . . shit, which way is north? Stephanie Kendall's directions say head north. Okay, where's the sun? No, that means west, or is that just during the day? Aaah, here we go—north. Okay, now make a left: "into main parking lot after passing Pollo Loco." Main parking lot, where are you? Okay. There ya are. "Check in with main office." Easy, two minutes max. Here are I come, you lucky kids!

"*Now,* who are you supposed to see?" a short woman in the school's main office asks a second time.

"Stephanie Kendall and I'm supposed to be in the cafeteria *right now*. I'm a guest speaker today and I'm already fifteen minutes late . . . Can't I just leave my driver's license with you?"

"No." She pauses slowly. "I'm afraid not. We have regulations. No one can enter the school grounds unless they're on the list. Kendall? Is that with a *K*? I don't see anything here. Larry." She turns to a kid at a typewriter behind her. "Larry, do you know a teacher by the name of Kendall? No, you don't?"

She turns back to me. "I just don't know. This is so odd. What grade does she teach?"

"Fifth. Fifth grade. Look, I really need to start my presentation. Is there anyone else you can ask?"

"Well, no wonder!" The woman looks up at me. "If you would've told me that in the very beginning, this whole mystery would've been solved. Did you hear that, Larry? No wonder we don't know any Kendall."

Okay, now I'm gonna go crazy. She knows something. Even Larry the student helper knows something. But me? I know nada. Let me in on your little secret, *please*!

"See," she explains, "this is Roosevelt *Intermediate*. You're looking for Roosevelt Elementary. What you need to do is . . ."

But I'm not listening anymore. I'm outta there. Running out of the office, down the hall, bumping into millions of cha-chas teetering on their super-high platform boots, knocking their super-shiny vinyl mini-backpacks that hang off their shoulders. I'm speeding so fast I can barely hear the barks of the hall monitor as he nips at my heels.

"Hey, slow down!" he yells after me. But *he's* too slow. I'm already in my car, out of the main gate, and heading onto Atlantic Boulevard, driving back down the main street. Where is that damn main parking lot? I see Pollo Loco, again. I'm back where I started from. Shit, I should've waited, should've listened to what that lady was saying. Main parking lot . . . main parking lot. Where is . . . Ah, right there! And there's this big kid with a shaved head, standing out front, flagging me down. *Yes, I see you.* I pull into the parking lot and he runs after my car.

"You're late!" He breathes heavily from his short run.

Dang, they start young.

"I know, I know. Here, can you help me with this?" I hand him a folder and a large plastic bottle of water. "Has everyone been waiting long?"

"Oh yeah, we didn't think you were gonna show up. Mrs. Kendall is inside reading your book to everyone."

"My book? You mean my stories?"

"Yeah, you wrote about the old lady and her owl, didn't you?"

"No, that's not me."

"Are you the one who lives in the purple house?"

"No, that's not me either."

"Well, I'll take you to the cafeteria, anyway."

We're rushing down another hallway when I see a sign.

"Is this the cafeteria?" I ask.

"Yeah, but go in through there." He points to a double door.

I enter through the doors and they bang shut behind me. I'm at the back of the cafeteria and all these little kids turn around. A hundred brown faces steaming pink from the midmorning heat, and there, on the stage, in my spot behind the podium, reading one of my poems from my book, is Stephanie Kendall. She smiles and waves not one, but both hands enthusiastically over her head.

"Oh, you made it!" she calls out. "We were so worried we gave you the wrong directions. Did we? Did we give you the wrong directions?"

Hey, there's an idea.

"Well," I tell her when I'm closer to the stage, "I didn't discover they were wrong till I was already way past Hayes Street and then I had to pull over and ask someone at a gas station."

All the kids remain quiet as if they are straining to hear some kind of conflict or argument take place between Stephanie Kendall and me. No such luck. Stephanie takes the full blame.

"Oh, dear, I feel horrible," she says.

"Well, it happens." I start to set my papers on the podium. "I just hate to keep the kids waiting." The whole cafeteria becomes noisy—paper rustling, binder rings snapping, and whispers, the kind of whispers that reek of judgment. It still gets to me. I know I should have dressed cooler.

"Oh, yes, of course." Stephanie pushes her long bangs out of her face and walks away from the podium. "I mean, of course not. Well, let's get you started. I was just reciting to the kids, you know, to prep them. They're very excited. What's that on your shirt?"

I look down and discover I spilled coffee on my chest. *Great.*

"Well." She looks away from the stain. "I'm sure it won't be noticeable once you're behind the podium. Oh, I'd like to introduce you, if you don't mind."

"Sure, I'm still setting up." I continue to arrange some notecards and my papers.

"Okay, children." Stephanie Kendall stands at the edge of the pullout stage and struggles to get their attention. "Shhhh . . . children! Luz, put the candy away now. There'll be no chocolate bars sold during this presentation. Okay, children. Listen up NOW! We have a very, very special guest, someone who drove a long way from the Westside to be with us here today. Children, we have with us today a writer, a poet, a Mexican-American writer who has overcome many obstacles in her life to get where she is today. I myself saw her read her poetry at a Chicana writers' conference about a year ago and that's why I've asked her here for Hispanic Heritage Month. She is a role model for you all. She is of your community. Marcel! *Cajete* now! As I was saying, children, she is a role model not just for Mexican-American children, but for all Hispanic children, children from Guatemala, from El Salvador, from—oh, you're ready? Okay, without any further delay, I present Michele Serros!"

And I stand there, behind the podium, smiling, while about five million kids, okay, maybe a hundred and fifty, brown kids, inner-city . . . well, you know, are waiting for me to start my talk. And my mouth starts to move and the words come out, the same words I've been repeating at least eight times a month, during extended lunches, after work, before school, on my few days off, and of all things, I still remember what Monica told me.

"Only loser artists still speak at schools," she said. And while she's up in Washington State leading a women's writing workshop in the countryside, enjoying the scent of jasmine and pine, I'm here, off the 710 Freeway inhaling manure from the nearby

Bandini plant and all the exhaust belched from every two-ton that roars by. Here again, in front of a cafeteria filled with elementary students, kids who could care less, seeing me only as a day's delay before their next math quiz. I read, talk, recount stories that are meant to inspire, entertain, educate. Personal conquests and the whole time I'm talking, reading these so-called heartfelt words from my so-called poetic soul, there are other more important issues that cloud my mind.

Eduardo Sanchez . . . man, he's got it going on! Artistic vision, success and he doesn't have to rely on all this Latino themed shit like me . . . plus he's so tall! How tall is he? In pictures he's always slouching like maybe he's insecure or something. I like shy boys. Oh, and those sexy sideburns! Okay, Blair Witch *wasn't all that scary, but I would never tell* him *that . . .*

Where am I? Okay, okay, still here, middle of the story. How could I possibly drift in and out like this? I need to stay focused. FOCUS! Did anyone notice? Good, looks like everyone is still paying attention. What's with that skinny kid and his backpack? I know I should've asked everyone to put their binders and backpacks under their seats before I started. God, I hate playing the disciplinarian. I'm the guest. I'm the role model. *I'm* the one giving back to my community and I don't want to put up with this shit. God, the kid with his backpack is really ruining this for me. Why can't he just pay attention to my story?!!

Ten more minutes to go. I wonder if I stopped reading now if the other teachers would notice. Only Stephanie Kendall knows for how long I was gonna read. Maybe my being late threw her off. Can I do a Q&A with fifth graders? Shit. They're getting antsy. What's with that teacher in the front row? Why is she twitching like that? Does she have to go to the bathroom? Go already! Okay, this is gonna be the last story and then I can start some kind of game. What kind of game? Game, game, game, something fun for fifth graders, something has to come to me!

I finish my story and turn over the paper that I was reading from. No applause, just a painful silence.

"And that's the end of that story." I let the cafeteria know that I'm done.

"Aren't you going to read again?" a voice in the back asks. It sounds old, a teacher's. "According to the schedule, you still have ten minutes."

"Well, I wanted to set some time aside for open dialogue."

Complete quiet. I hear another two-ton roar by on the freeway.

"I mean, questions and answers," I explain.

More silence. This little girl, a flacita, whispers to her friend and they both laugh. What are they laughing at? Are they laughing at me? I didn't say anything funny. What's so funny?

"Well." I try to ignore them. "What I want to do is, uh, talk a little about what it is like to be a writer. Does anyone have any questions?"

More silence followed by sounds of binder rings snapping.

"No? Well, uh, I had this game in mind that I think would be fun to play. It will involve everyone and it's like a word game and sometimes when I am alone I . . ." I start shifting around the papers on the podium. I look at the clock over the American flag. I smile at Mrs. Kendall. I look at the clock again. *Help me. Damn it! Please?*

"Wow." I scan the audience and smile. "There are just so many handsome young men and pretty girls in the audience! You're not all in the fifth grade are you? You all look like you're at least in the sixth."

More silence. I see one of the teachers frown. Man, NO sense of humor!

All of a sudden . . . the bell! Oh yes! That glorious sound, that savior from failure. I can't believe what it still represents to me, even years after graduating from grade school. The bell. Thank you, thank you, thank you!

"Okay, kids. Kids, before you leave for recess"—Mrs. Kendall takes over—"we need to thank Miss Serros for coming here today. She is a writer. A Mexican-American writer and everything in her life has been a struggle for her. My class, I want everyone to line up and give her a high five."

"But, Mrs. Kendall, it's already recess!"

"No! You will get in line and high-five her. Everyone, now! Two lines—boys here, girls over here."

"But, Mrs. Kendall!"

"No!" she screams. "Get in line and high-five her, NOW!"

And while the rest of the cafeteria runs out onto the playground, Mrs. Kendall's class lines up to grant me high fives. Now, everybody knows that high fives are a gesture denoting excitement or achievement, shared by enthusiastic participating parties. But what I get are sweaty fifth-grade, germ-infested hostile swaps. Sharp stinging slaps across my palm—hard, angry, defiant. "It's 'cause of YOU, Miss Mexican-American writer," these high fives accuse, "that we're gonna be late for recess! It is because of YOU I don't get dibs on the tether ball! Thanks a fudging lot, Miss Struggling Mexican-American Writer!"

I smile at each child and I switch my hands every so often to lessen the pain and break up the monotony. Thirty-two pairs of hands wait impatiently in line to smack my own and finally, after the seemingly endless five-minute formality, the last kid slaps his small brown fingers across my hand and races out.

Stephanie Kendall approaches me. "Well," she exhales. "That was nice. But, I don't understand. They're usually so excited about visitors. I mean, usually they don't even want to leave for recess. They just want to be *near* a guest speaker."

I start to collect my things from the podium.

"Do you know Eva Perez, the Peruvian poet?" she asks.

"I've never heard of her," I lie.

"Really? She's Hispanic."

"Yeah, well."

"She was such a hit just last week. The kids just loved her."

"Great." *Thanks a lot, Stephanie. You can stop anytime.*

"I mean, I've been teaching here for eight years and I've never witnessed anything like when Eva Perez visited. Some of the kids even started a fan club for her."

"That's wonderful."

"Yes." Stephanie Kendall laughs. "She's quite a woman. She's really great with kids."

Oh, and I'm not? "Well, they're really wonderful kids," I tell her. "So attentive. I'd love to come back." *Yeah, right.*

"Say." She looks at her watch. "Would you like to stay for lunch? We always have our guest speakers eat in the teachers' lounge and I'd love you to meet some of the other teachers."

What's this? The teachers' lounge? During the entire twelve-year duration of my formal education I'd taken only mere peeks of the teachers' lounge. One time in the eleventh grade when I was on my way to the library, I saw Father Sanders loosen his collar and light up a cigarette that was *on a holder,* and another time, in the seventh grade over at Rio Del Valle Junior High, I caught Ol' Lady Oily Hair, our home-economics teacher, eating SpaghettiOs out of the can. And it wasn't even heated! Can you believe that? I should've demanded a recall on the C-plus she gave me! More than anything I wanted the inside edition of the teachers' lounge, to kick it with the academic heads, but to experience it with Stephanie Kendall? No way.

"Oh, that really sounds so pleasant," I tell her. "But I really should get to work. I work way over in Santa Monica and I don't wanna be late. That's one thing that's important to me—being on time."

"Should you make a call?"

"Nah." I wave my hand. "They're pretty flexible. Besides, my boss knows that right now writing is my main focus."

"Uh-huh." She isn't really paying attention anymore. "Well, that's a shame," she says. "I really wanted you to meet the other teachers and I wanted to talk about some of your stories. I have some suggestions."

"Suggestions?"

"Yeah, just a few minor improvements. You know, in college I majored in English with an emphasis in Latin American policy."

"Well, I'm not from Latin America. I'm from here."

"Oh, that's right. I guess I'm still thinking of Eva Perez. Well, I can at least walk you to your car."

My car suddenly couldn't seem farther away, and while we cross the field of empty metal fold-up chairs in the cafeteria, all I can think about was how evil Stephanie Kendall is. How can she be talking to me this way? Doesn't she know I know I sucked? Doesn't she know I would feel shitty knowing how popular another poet was with her students? I immediately hate Stephanie Kendall. I damn her to a life of cafeteria poetry readings and call for the powers that be to create southeast winds over the Bandini manure plant. There is nothing Stephanie Kendall can say or do to make up for her evil. Nothing. Just then a particular smell hits me and no, it's not from the Bandini plant.

"Wow." I inhale the aroma. "Is that coming from the kitchen? Is that what I think it is?"

"Yes, it is," she brags in a singsong type of way.

"Seriously?" I ask her. "Is that what they're serving today? I mean, it's not someone's lunch they're heating up for themselves in the microwave, is it?"

"Oh, no, we have it every Tuesday," she promises. "Sometimes we have so much of it, they serve it again on Wednesday."

"Well." I check my own watch. "I guess I can be a little bit late to work. I mean, a person has to eat."

"Great!" Stephanie Kendall links arms with me. "I'm so happy you can eat with us." She leads me toward the aroma and into the teachers' lounge.

"Hey," I ask her. "Did Eva Perez visit on a Tuesday?"

"Actually, if my memory serves me right, I think she came on—wait let me see, she came on a Monday morning. Yes, now that I think of it, it was a Monday."

"What do they serve on Monday?"

"Green-bean casserole and tunafish salad, why?"

"Oh, nothing." I smile smugly to myself as I take a plastic tray from the stack. I follow Stephanie Kendall down the food line and eye the miniature chicken pot pies that line the counter. I can see the thick yellow gravy bubbling out of the burned cracked crust and take the largest one. They smell *so* good and I realize it's been years since my own wonderful Mexican mother heated up a traditional frozen chicken pot pie for me.

"Puedo tener más . . . más salsa?" I ask the server in a hair net across from me.

"You want more . . . gravy?" she asks nervously.

"Uh, yeah."

"I heard your stories, from the kitchen."

"Oh, really?"

"Yeah, I stopped what I was doing 'cause I didn't want to miss a word. They were really nice. I enjoyed them a lot."

"Oh, thanks."

She ladles more gravy from a separate basin and drowns my pie with it. Suddenly my getting to work on time and my being late to Roosevelt Elementary and presenting a sucky poetry reading in a coffee-stained shirt doesn't matter. In just the last hour I finished a job created by me—with my own thoughts, words, opinions, with my *own* name. I created something out of what I was told I could never do. The so-called obstacles in my life that so many people tried to make me feel ashamed about suddenly seem less important. So what if I'm still in junior college after six years? Big deal I'm not fluent in Spanish and that I still wear a corduroy smock to pay my rent. Here is someone telling me they actually stopped what they were doing just to hear what I had to say. It's pretty cool having people listen to what you want heard. No, it's *very* cool. I begin to feel this incredibly intense sense of excitement and happiness. I look up at the woman and smile. She smiles back. And then, more than at any other time during my fledgling career as an aspiring Chicana role model, I sorta, in a way, actually feel like one.

About the Author

Michele Serros was born in 1966 in Oxnard, California. She loves tacos from Titos and making prank phone calls. She credits her parents, Beatrice and George, as the primary role models in her life.